Enrollment Form

☐ *Yes!* I WANT TO BE A *Privileged Woman.*

Enclosed is one *PAGES & PRIVILEGES*™ Proof of Purchase from any Harlequin or Silhouette book currently for sale in stores (Proofs of Purchase are found on the back pages of books) and the store cash register receipt. Please enroll me in *PAGES & PRIVILEGES*™. Send my Welcome Kit and FREE Gifts -- and activate my FREE benefits -- immediately.

More great gifts and benefits to come like these luxurious Truly Lace and L'Effleur gift baskets.

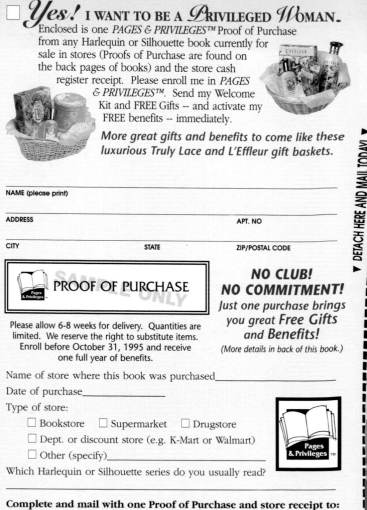

NAME (please print)

ADDRESS   APT. NO

CITY   STATE   ZIP/POSTAL CODE

PROOF OF PURCHASE

Pages & Privileges™

SAMPLE ONLY

Please allow 6-8 weeks for delivery. Quantities are limited. We reserve the right to substitute items. Enroll before October 31, 1995 and receive one full year of benefits.

NO CLUB! NO COMMITMENT!
Just one purchase brings you great Free Gifts and Benefits!

(More details in back of this book.)

Name of store where this book was purchased_____

Date of purchase_____

Type of store:

☐ Bookstore ☐ Supermarket ☐ Drugstore

☐ Dept. or discount store (e.g. K-Mart or Walmart)

☐ Other (specify)_____

Which Harlequin or Silhouette series do you usually read?

_____

Pages & Privileges™

Complete and mail with one Proof of Purchase and store receipt to:

U.S.: *PAGES & PRIVILEGES*™, P.O. Box 1960, Danbury, CT 06813-1960

Canada: *PAGES & PRIVILEGES*™, 49-6A The Donway West, P.O. 813, North York, ON M3C 2E8

PRINTED IN U.S.A

▶ DETACH HERE AND MAIL TODAY! ▶

"You think we should *what?*"

David was gaping at C.J.

"We should get married wearing regular clothes. On the beach." She paused. "And barefoot."

"And then what? Buy a '69 Volkswagen Bug, move to a commune and grow marijuana? C.J., this is the nineties. This is Chicago. People like us don't get married barefoot on beaches. They wear white gowns and black tuxes and they walk down aisles...."

C.J. was starting to get an inkling that David's idea of the perfect wedding might not mesh with her own.

"That's exactly my point—that everyone does the same thing. I just don't want a typical wedding. I don't want to wear a veil and a flowing white dress."

"What do you want to wear?" he asked.

She'd thought something short and black, but the look on his face stopped her from telling him that....

LOOP QUIZ: HOW TRADITIONAL A BRIDE DO YOU WANT TO BE?

Question one: You've decided to get married. Do you:

a) Begin planning more than a year in advance, looking at every formal hall you can find. You're going to be princess for a day!

b) Find a funky party space. No meddling mother-in-law is going to tell *you* how to have fun.

c) Book a flight to Las Vegas.

Question two: Your dress will make you look like:

a) Princess Diana…before she realized her prince was a toad.

b) A Betsey Johnson runway model.

c) Dress smesh!

Question three: Your wedding party consists of:

a) So many attendants that the head table may crash from the collective weight.

b) The only sister still talking to you once the family realized there's no reception at "The Crystal Pavillion Wedding Palace."

c) The Priscilla lookalike, big hair and all!

Question four: The most touching musical moment will be:

a) The sounds of "Daddy's Little Girl" played by a tasteful ensemble.

b) The deejay playing Dave Edmonds singing "I Knew the Bride When She Used To Rock and Roll."

c) The Elvis impersonator who married you croons "Love Me Tender."

Score: Give yourself three points for every A answer, two points for every B answer and one point for every C answer.

If you scored 10-12: You are THE traditional bride. Don't forget to request a Viennese table!

If you scored 6-8: You'll have a wild time, but won't forget to toss the bouquet.

If you scored 4-5: Viva Las Vegas!

Remember: it's YOUR DAY and you can do whatever you want to. The important thing is that you're in love. May all your endings be happy ones.

Lucia Macro

Getting Hitched: CJ

WENDY CORSI STAUB

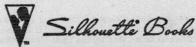

Published by Silhouette Books

America's Publisher of Contemporary Romance

SILHOUETTE BOOKS

ISBN 0-373-20212-1

GETTING HITCHED: CJ

WHO'S WHO

C. J. CLARKE:
The wedding date's been set but life seems more complicated than ever! Not only is C.J.'s mother turning her wedding into a circus, but her usually predictable fiancé has suddenly gone crazy. And on top of that, her own monstrous secret is eating away at her mercilessly. Will she and David make it down the aisle in one piece?

DAVID GRIFFIN:
It never used to bother C.J. that David was the strong, silent type, but now she won't stop until she figures out what's going on inside that cute head of his. But doesn't she know the more she pushes him to open up, the more she's pushing him away?

SEAMUS DOWD:
Decides trying to adjust to life without potato chips, pizza and nicotine isn't worth it. And neither is being a paper pusher from nine to five. So Seamus quits his job and moves in with his lover—what's the *point* of not living the way you want to?

LILA CLARKE:
Now that her only daughter is finally tying the knot, Lila Clarke just can't do enough planning for the big day. But she can't figure out why C.J. doesn't want big bows or a frilly lace gown...or even her mother's help!

FAWN GRIFFIN:
David's stepmother and Lila's old friend, Fawn wants C.J. and David's wedding to be the event of the year. Who cares if *they* don't want a big hoopla? Isn't that what getting married is all about?

For Kim Byham Powell,
my true-blue, life-long friend,
whose wedding to Bill on 9/3/94
came off without a hitch...
well, almost!
(P.S. Bill regained consciousness before the vows!)

And for Mark
with joyful memories of Getting Hitched
on October 26, 1991.

With special thanks to David Staub,
who rescued the elusive Chapter Ten
from the depths of computer limbo.

One

C.J. woke with a jolt and looked around to get her bearings. She was in her own bedroom in her apartment in Chicago's Loop neighborhood, and her fiancé, David Griffin, was snoring softly beside her. She glanced at the clock by the bed—5:11 a.m.

This wasn't the first time that she had been startled awake by a bad dream. It had been happening a lot these days. She had so much on her mind....

It had been over a year since C.J. had spontaneously quit her job as production assistant at WZZ TV in Chicago.

Over a year since her boyfriend, David Griffin, had unexpectedly become her fiancé.

Both of those things had come to pass on the same day—her birthday—which also happened to be the day she had received the results of her HIV test—negative. Thank God.

C.J. and David had decided to wait a year before getting married. After all, she was unemployed when David proposed, and hardly in a position to plan a wedding. She had to find a job—*any* job.

Luckily, one had dropped into her lap only days after she'd quit WZZ. For the past year, she had been working as a temporary production assistant to Harry Cribbe, the documentary filmmaker whose apartment David had been subletting. Actually, David was *still* subletting the apartment, because when Harry had returned from Europe, he'd had his very pregnant girlfriend/assistant, Ilse, in tow. The two of them, Harry and Ilse, had rented a two-bedroom apartment together and were now the parents of a round-faced little boy named Harry Sven.

C.J. had been perfectly content working as Harry's assistant, although a few weeks ago, Ilse had gone back to her old job working for Harry, and now C.J. was out of work once again. Oh, Harry and Ilse *had* offered to hire her as their nanny. Little Harry Sven was adorable and all, but C.J. didn't exactly feel up to spending all day, every day, alone with him.

Not that she knew exactly what she *did* feel like doing all day, every day.

So basically, she was back where she had started a year ago—out of work, with no clear idea of what she wanted to do.

And this time, she also had a wedding to plan. She couldn't put it off any longer.

Actually, a couple of months ago, in June, she and David had decided it was time to set a date and get their plans underway. But then they'd gotten the horrible middle-of-the-night phone call that had postponed everything.

C.J.'s younger brother, Kyle, had been involved in a horrible accident in which his friend Maggie had been killed. Kyle had been pretty banged-up himself, and it had taken two months for him to recover. C.J. hadn't had the heart to make wedding plans in the midst of what her brother was going through.

Now Kyle was almost back to normal physically, although emotionally, he was no longer the lighthearted kid brother C.J. had grown up with.

All summer, ever since that phone call, she had been haunted by nightmares about car wrecks. In some of them, it was Kyle who had been killed. In others, it was David, or one of her parents.

Whenever she woke up in the middle of the night, her heart racing and her whole body trembling, David held her and stroked her head and assured her that it was only a dream, it wasn't real.

This time, the nightmare that had woken her hadn't been about an accident. But that didn't mean it wasn't frightening.

In the beginning, the dream had been about nothing in particular—one of those going-nowhere dreams in which you went about your regular, real-life routine. In it, C.J. had slept in on a Saturday morning, and when she got up, she'd realized she had her period. She had stuck her hair in a ponytail and put on the baggy gray sweatpants she always wore in real life when she was bloated. She was lounging around her apartment eating a big submarine sandwich with lots of raw onions on it, when the doorbell rang. A limousine driver was standing there, and so was her mother, who was all dressed up in a turquoise mother-of-the-bride outfit. Lila Clarke had started yelling at C.J., asking why she wasn't ready.

And C.J., her mouth full of sandwich, had asked, "Ready for what?"

"Your wedding—it's your wedding day, Clara Joy! You have to be at the church in fifteen minutes. Everyone's waiting."

And C.J. had panicked, because how could she have forgotten something so important? And how could she get ready in fifteen minutes? She didn't have a wedding gown; she *did* have her period—and onion breath.

Calm down. It wasn't real, she told herself now, as she lay there in her quiet, dark bedroom. But she couldn't shake the frantic feeling she'd had in the dream.

"David?" she whispered, tapping his shoulder.

No reaction.

"David?"

There. His snoring was tapering off.

"David!"

"Wha . . . ?" He rolled toward her.

"OhmyGod."

"Huh?"

"I said, oh . . . my . . . God."

"What happened? Another nightmare about the accident?"

"It was a dream, but not about that." C.J. was sitting up now, shaking her head. "David, we're engaged. I'm unemployed again."

"So what else is new?" he asked, showing a trace of his trademark broad, crinkly grin.

"I have to get busy." She swung her bare legs out from under the tangled covers.

"Now? It's the middle of the night."

"It is not. It's practically dawn. And it's not like there's time to waste. I mean, I have to get a job. And I have to plan a wedding. How can I have been sitting around twiddling my thumbs for all this time?"

David made a sound that was a yawn and a sigh rolled into one. "C.J., you haven't been twiddling your thumbs. You haven't even been around lately."

Which was true. The same week Ilse had come back to work for Harry, David had left for a ten-day banking seminar in New York. C.J. had let her old roommate Becky talk her into a two-week visit to the small Iowa town where she now lived. C.J. had planned to spend that time figuring out what she wanted to do next, careerwise, and thumbing through bridal magazines.

Instead, she hadn't given much thought to either. She and Becky had gone shopping almost every day, seen every summer blockbuster movie that was playing in Des Moines and ridden horses on Becky's uncle's farm. And they spent the warm July evenings rocking on Becky's front porch swing, listening to crickets and talking about the past. It was infinitely more comforting than the future.

When C.J. had returned to Chicago last week, David had taken a few days off and they'd bummed around the city together, going to museums or the beach, depending on the weather. It was one of those sticky Julys when the temperature reached the mid-nineties every day, rain or shine.

Humidity made C.J. cranky. The only good thing about it was that she didn't feel like eating much besides watermelon and salads, and she was able to sweat off at least five pounds without any conscious effort.

Of course, she still had about forty more to go before she'd be in the normal weight range for her height.

Every time David brought up the subject of setting a date for their wedding or he mentioned her unemployed status, C.J. had snapped at him that she didn't feel like talking about it.

"It's too hot for conflict," she kept saying, even as David, in true David form, repeatedly protested that he wasn't trying to bring up conflict—he only wanted to discuss their future.

C.J. would give him a pointed look, he would drop the subject and invariably, they'd end up in bed together shortly after. Neither of them had an air-conditioned apartment, but somehow, the dark, sultry nights seemed to fuel, rather than put a damper on, their lust.

But sometime last night, the temperature had dropped to the mid-sixties for the first time in weeks. C.J. vaguely remembered waking in the wee hours, fumbling at the foot of the bed for the comforter and pulling it up over the sheet.

Now a cool breeze fluttered the filmy summer white curtains in her bedroom window, and she shivered in her shorty nightgown as she got out of bed and stood.

"Where are you going?" David asked, reaching out and catching her fingers in his.

She shrugged. "I don't know. I just feel like I can't lie around one moment longer."

"It's—" he lifted his head to glance at the bedside clock "—five o'clock in the morning. You're *supposed* to be lying around. The whole *world* is lying around right now."

"Not the whole world. In London, it's, like, practically afternoon."

"London? What does that have to do with anything?"

She shrugged and slipped her hand from his grasp. It was too early to make excuses for a non sequitur. And besides, she had work to do.

She went over to her dresser and took a sweatshirt from the bottom drawer.

"What are you doing now?" David asked, watching her from the bed.

"I'm cold."

"How can you be co—Hey, you're right. It really *did* cool off. Guess WZZ's new meteorologist knows what he's talking about, huh? And you said he was a big lug-head."

"He *is* a big lug-head. Seamus told me."

Seamus was C.J.'s dearest friend and current roommate. Until she'd quit her job, he was also a co-worker. He was still an assistant producer at WZZ and kept C.J. apprised of the latest gossip about insipid anchorwoman Bunny Bartholomew and the rest of the gang. The best news C.J. had heard from him was back in May, when he'd told her that her old boss, Leonora Nagle, had been fired. It was about time they figured out that the woman did absolutely nothing.

C.J. pulled the sweatshirt over her head. The soft fleece settled against her goose-pimpled bare arms. It felt odd. She hadn't worn long sleeves in months. Socks, either, she realized, as she slipped a pair over her chilly toes.

She swiftly ran a brush through her long, brown, spiral-permed hair and snapped a scrunchy around it to keep it out of her face. Then she padded across the floor and opened the door to the hallway.

David made a rustling sound in the bed, snuggling into the comforter. "Wake me up at seven," he murmured.

"The alarm's still set."

She paused in the doorway, then went back over to the bed. Leaning over David, she planted a gentle kiss on the sandy-reddish hair and ran a fingertip along his tanned, freckled cheek.

"What was that for?"

"Nothing. Just—I love you," she said, and left the room.

It still felt wonderful to say those three little words. And she did, whenever she felt like it, now that she could. For so many months, before they'd gotten engaged, she'd just thought them, afraid to voice them because she hadn't expected David to say them back.

That seemed so long ago.

And so did her fling with Dig Lawrence, male model—and egotistical jerk. It had happened at a rocky time in her relationship with David, when she wanted more commitment than he was willing to give. C.J. had let her resentment build until—boom! The first time he left town on a business trip, she'd cheated on him. She hadn't intended to do it. Hell, she couldn't even *remember* doing it.

Every time she thought of that horrible morning over a year ago when she'd woken up with a monstrous hangover to find a blissfully snoring Dig in her bed, she felt a twinge of nausea. How could she have done such a horrible thing to David?

On and off over the past year, she'd played with the idea of telling him about it, especially when it occurred to her that Dig Lawrence lived life in the fast lane, and who was to say that he didn't have the HIV virus? But then she had tested negative, and immediately after she found out her results, David sprung the engagement on her . . . and it was too late to come clean with him.

So she continued to pretend the episode with Dig had never happened. And to pray that David would never find out about it. And to try to overcome the still-nagging guilt over what she had done.

And to think that someday, when David had been her husband for a while—maybe years—she would finally clear her conscience and tell him. And he would say that what she had done was no big deal. That it didn't matter.

Someday.

But for now, it was a secret—one that unfortunately kept poking its ugly presence into C.J.'s thoughts and churning up guilt and regrets. Still. Even though six months ago, she had had a second HIV test and come up negative once again. So there was really no reason to dwell on the thing with Dig any longer. She was fine, and David would never have to know.

In the kitchen, C.J. turned on the light and noted the two black-stemmed crystal wineglasses in the sink.

Seamus and Chad must have come back last night after C.J. and David went to bed. Sometimes, her roommate spent the night at Chad's place, but usually they came here. Seamus had told C.J. that Chad's apartment made him feel uncomfortable. C.J. didn't blame him. It was where Chad had lived with his lover, who had died of AIDs a few years back.

Chad had already been HIV positive when Seamus met him over a year ago. Seamus hadn't found out about his own status—also positive—until they'd started dating.

At first he'd been devastated, and so had C.J. Now Seamus was learning, somehow, to live with the threat of dying. And so far he'd been healthy. He spent a lot of time with Chad, and the two of them seemed to draw strength from each other. C.J. couldn't help thinking that it was ironic that the very thing that seemed to draw Seamus and his lover together would eventually tear them apart.

She couldn't imagine how it must feel, knowing that in the not-so-distant future, you—or the person you loved—were going to die. What if something happened to David? What if he were sick and she knew she were going to lose him?

C.J. couldn't bear the thought and pushed it out of her head.

She sighed and ran hot water into the two glasses. She squirted dishwashing liquid into them and let them soak. Then she washed her hands thoroughly with soap, telling herself she wasn't being overly paranoid.

Logically, intellectually, C.J. believed what medical research said—that you couldn't catch AIDs from touching a glass an infected person had used. But a tiny, emotional sliver in the back of her mind was worried. What if they discovered someday that they'd been wrong?

She hated feeling squeamish about living with an HIV-positive roommate. She'd never want Seamus to suspect that she worried sometimes that he'd taken a swig directly from the carton of milk in the refrigerator or dipped a spoon into the peanut butter, licked it and dipped it again. Those had been habits of his before he'd ever discovered his status.

Part of C.J. was anxious to move out, to get a place with David at last, and not just because she wouldn't have to face the reality of the HIV virus on a daily basis anymore. She was ready to move into their own home—to start a new life with David.

But another part of her was a little wistful about leaving Seamus. He'd been living with her ever since Becky and her other roommate, Jessica, had moved out last spring. C.J. had grown more attached to him than ever, even though they no longer worked together. She couldn't bear the thought of losing him. And it was inevitable.

Reality.

It always came back to that.

She sighed and measured coffee into a filter, then turned on the faucet and waited for the water to go from luke-warm to cold. It had the algae smell that Lake Michigan always got in August, and C.J. wrinkled her nose. After a minute or so, she realized that it wasn't going to get much colder than tepid—it never did in summer—so she filled the pot and poured the water into the coffeemaker.

Then she went into the living room to hunt for yesterday's *Tribune*. Usually there weren't many jobs listed in the Classifieds on a weekday, but it couldn't hurt to check.

Belatedly, she remembered that she hadn't bought the paper. She'd been meaning to, but she'd spent the day cleaning the apartment, and by the time David got out of work, she'd been too tired to go out. So they'd stayed in, ordered a pizza and watched a lineup of sitcom reruns on TV.

Oh, well. She'd go get today's paper as soon as David left for work.

For now, she'd concentrate on the wedding instead.

She looked around for the batch of bridal magazines her mother had mailed her back in May, before the accident.

Lila Clarke was obviously beside herself with joy at the prospect of her only daughter's wedding. C.J. had always suspected her mother assumed she'd never get married. After all, who would want a chubbette for a wife?

David does, C.J. retorted to a mental image of her perennially tight-lipped mother. *David loves me just the way I am.*

That was what he said.

And C.J. believed him.

She really did.

But—she located the stack of magazines under the couch—deep down, she knew that David wouldn't exactly be *despondent* if C.J. lost fifty pounds and floated down the aisle on their wedding day looking like the radiant cover model pictured on the top magazine.

For the first time, she entertained the notion that maybe part of the reason she was putting off planning her wedding was that she was fat. Still.

All her life, she'd put off losing weight, although she'd always halfheartedly been on some type of diet. In high school, she'd told herself she'd get thin ''for real'' in college. In college, having picked up the proverbial ''freshman ten'' pounds, and then some, she'd told herself she'd get thin when she'd graduated and fallen in love.

Then she met David and finally accepted that someone could actually love her the way she was. And from then on, at the back of her mind, she'd always been thinking that there was only one last motivation to lose the weight: her wedding day.

She'd never wanted to be one of those overweight brides you saw in the Sunday papers. Oh, they were always rosy and happy, but they tended to look so…well, so *big.* Swathed in yards and yards of tulle and taffeta, they dwarfed their typically slim, tuxedo-clad grooms, who always seemed to be smiling feebly.

It was so unfair, C.J. thought now, that the men got to wear black to their weddings.

White was hardly slimming. In fact, the only white items in C.J.'s closet were the blouses she'd occasionally worn to work. Most of the time, to David's chagrin, she was clad in black from head to toe.

She took the heavy stack of bridal magazines into the kitchen and dumped them on the table. Then she took out a mug, slid the coffeepot out of the way and filled her cup directly from the still-trickling machine.

She sipped the steaming black liquid, winced and went to the refrigerator for skim milk. She dumped some into the cup and mentally wrote a fraction of a fat gram on her ever-present daily tally. Her goal for today would be ten grams or less.

Make that five, she thought, thinking "wedding" again.

Taking her coffee to the table, she sat on a chair cross-legged and reached for the first magazine.

A quick thumb-through told her what she'd already suspected. None of the flowing white dresses appealed to her, and none of them would be flattering on her. Most of them were made for mannequin brides who were hipless and breastless and thighless. Not to mention that most of the gowns were far too fussy, with sequins and beads, frills and poufs, for C.J.'s taste. Didn't any designer make a simple *dress?*

Apparently not, she concluded, tossing the magazine aside, disgusted.

She reached for the next one. *Midwestern Bridal Fancies.* Her mother had stuck a yellow Post-it note on the glossy cover. It read, "Clara Joy, turn to page 202 and you'll see the perfect dress for you. I can picture you in it already! Love, Mom."

C.J. rolled her eyes, took a sip of coffee and leafed through the magazine until she reached page 202. She nearly gagged at what she saw there. A whiter-than-white, elaborate confection of a dress that included yards of lace, dozens of appliqués, beads, bows, sequins, and a ninety-mile scallop-edged train. Oh, God—and a bustle.

Her mother had stuck another Post-it to that page. It read, "Clara Joy, I think this would be perfect for you— without the bustle, of course. Perhaps a hoopskirt instead? Love, Mom."

Without the bustle.

C.J. rolled her eyes.

What her mother meant was that she, C.J., had a built-in bustle in the form of a gigantic butt.

A hoopskirt?

Who did her mother think she was, Scarlett O'Hara?

C.J. looked at the picture again, noting the way the sparkly bodice hugged the model's teensy-weensy waistline.

Sighing, she tore the page out of the magazine.

She glanced at it again.

Then she ripped it into tiny pieces and threw them into the trash.

"You think that we should *what?*" David had stopped buttoning his starched white shirt and was gaping at C.J.

"I said, I think that we should get married wearing regular clothes. On the beach." She paused. "And barefoot."

"And then what? Buy a '69 Volkswagen Bug, move to a commune and grow marijuana?" He shook his head, finished buttoning his shirt and slung a navy blue tie patterned with red paisley around his neck. "I mean, Jeez, C.J., this isn't the Age of Aquarius. This is the nineties. This is Chicago. People don't get married barefoot on beaches."

"Sure they do."

"Not people like us."

"What do 'people like us' do?"

"I don't know—they wear white gowns and black tuxes and they walk down aisles...."

"And someone sings 'We've Only Just Begun,' and the photographer climbs around taking a million pictures and people throw rice—"

"Birdseed. They don't do rice anymore."

"How do you know?"

"I just know. And anyway, we can't get married barefoot on the beach because we're going to have a winter wedding. I'm not waiting until next summer to get married."

Despite his refusal to seriously consider her idea, C.J. felt a pleasant little glow. He didn't want to wait until next summer. He wanted her to be his wife as soon as possible. *His wife.* The notion still sent flutters through her almost-empty stomach.

"Listen," David said, "I've been trying to bring up our wedding for days now, and you always change the subject. Why is it that you suddenly want to discuss it now, when I'm late for work? This really isn't a terrific time for a logical discussion."

A logical discussion. It was such a David thing to say. The man was nothing if not logical. It was one of the things she loved about him—except that sometimes, his levelheaded, sensible attitudes frustrated her. Like now, when she was starting to get an inkling that David's idea of the perfect wedding might not mesh with her own.

She flopped on her stomach on the bed, watching as he tugged his tie knot up and settled it in the V between the crisp points of his collar. He inspected his image in the mirror and frowned. "Did I tie this too short?"

C.J. peered at it. "Yes. Wait—no. I don't know, maybe."

He shot her an exasperated look.

"Just leave it. You look fine. You *always* look fine. Anyway, getting back to the wedding—" David sighed. She ignored him and continued. "I *know* what people like us do when they get married. That's my exact point—that everyone does the same thing. Don't you want our wedding to be different?"

"Different, how?" He sat on the edge of the bed, bent over and slipped a shoehorn into the heel of his right wing tip.

"I just don't want a typical wedding. I don't want to wear a veil and a flowing white dress, whatever."

"What do you want to wear?" he asked, glancing up. His eyebrows were raised and he seemed distracted, momentarily, from tying his shoe.

She'd thought something short and black, but the look on his face stopped her from telling him that.

"I don't know. Something different," she said vaguely instead. "But that's not the issue. I think our whole wedding should be different. I want people to remember it forever."

He finished putting on his other shoe, stood and slipped his suit coat off the hanger. "*We'll* remember it forever, C.J.—isn't that what matters? Don't make such a big deal out of planning this thing. I remember what my sisters were like for months before their weddings." He shuddered, then bent toward C.J. and gave her a quick kiss on the cheek. "The important thing is we're going to get married, right? Listen, I've got to get going."

She shrugged and followed him into the hall. "There's coffee."

"No time. I'm late." He stooped to pick up his briefcase from the floor by the door.

"What time do you think you'll get out tonight?"

"I don't know. I'm still trying to get caught up from being out of the office for the past few weeks. I'll call you later." He kissed her again on the cheek.

"Okay. Bye." C.J. shut the door behind him. Down the hall, from behind the closed door to Seamus's room, she could hear a radio playing and the low, rumbling sound of male voices. He and Chad must be getting ready for work.

She padded back into the kitchen and refilled her coffee cup. She was plunking herself down in the chair again when Seamus came into the kitchen.

"Well, well, well. Aren't *we* up early today."

"Hi," C.J. said. "Where's Chad?"

"Trying to decide whether he wants to borrow my dark brown socks, which don't quite match his suit, or go sockless."

"To the D.A.'s office?"

Seamus shrugged, poured some coffee into a mug and lit a cigarette. "What's with the vast assortment of bridal mags?" he asked, sitting down across from her.

"I'm trying to convince myself that I want a conventional wedding with all the trimmings."

"What else is there?"

She shook her head. "I wouldn't mind getting married barefoot on the beach, but David wasn't crazy about that."

"No!" Seamus said wryly. "Really?"

She was instantly defensive. "He may be a banker, Seamus, but he's not *that* conventional. Not usually, anyway." Seamus raised his eyebrows, and before he could point out that she was always saying David was too conventional, she went on, "But I was thinking maybe we could rent one of those big empty lofts in the warehouse district and hire an alternative band or something. What do you think?"

Seamus exhaled a thin stream of smoke and got up to tap his ashes into the sink. "I think I'm really thankful I'm not heterosexual," he said, running water to wash them down the drain. "I'd hate to have to have a wedding. Hoopla is such a drag."

"Speaking of *drag*, you'd better not back out on being my 'man of honor.' You promised."

"I wouldn't dream of backing out. But I didn't think you wanted me there in drag," he teased.

"If my mother has her way, my half of the wedding party will be decked out in rainbow pastels with hoopskirts and parasols."

"Oh? Well, just remember, mint green is my best color," Seamus said, and inhaled his cigarette again.

C.J. laughed. They were only kidding, of course. Not about Seamus being her man of honor, but about his wearing a dress. Although, she'd love to see the look on her mother's face if she informed her that Seamus was going to dress like "one of the girls."

Chad came into the kitchen dressed in an expensive charcoal-colored suit, his glossy black hair combed straight back.

"Well?" Seamus asked, looking down at his friend's feet.

Chad lifted a pant leg to reveal bare ankles. "I couldn't go with the dark brown socks. Too tacky."

"Don't you think wearing dress shoes without socks is even tackier?" Seamus asked.

"I'm going to stop off and buy some socks on the way to the office."

"I don't know how many times I've told you that you should keep more of your things here," Seamus said, after draining the rest of his coffee and plunking his cup into the sink. "You can have a drawer in my dresser. Hell, take *two* drawers."

"That's all right."

"That's *not* all right. I'm getting so tired of going through this with him every morning when he gets dressed," Seamus told C.J., rolling his eyes like an exasperated spouse.

"I know how it is," she said, again thinking about how wonderful it was going to be when she and David lived together at last.

Seamus stubbed out his cigarette in the sink and looked at Chad. "Are you ready?"

"Do I have time for a quick cup of coffee?"

"No."

"Okay. Then I'm ready."

"Bye, guys," C.J. called after them as they headed for the door.

As soon as they left, she noticed how silent the apartment was. She stretched, looked at the clock and debated whether she should take a shower or go lie on the couch and watch the rest of "Good Morning America."

Get moving, she commanded herself. *You've already decided it's time to take action. You have a lot to do.*

But somehow, both planning a wedding and trying to find a job had lost their appeal.

You have no choice.

Sighing, she stood and headed down the hall for the shower.

Her first stop was the newsstand on the corner. She grabbed both the *Tribune* and the *Sun-Times* and this week's issue of *Chicago Now,* the weekly alternative newspaper where Becky had once worked as a personal ad taker.

Now Becky, lucky Becky, was settled back in Iowa again, where she was feature editor of the local paper and happily dating her old high school sweetheart.

For a while, C.J. had assumed that her friend would end up marrying Michael Max, the guy she'd started dating here in Chicago. But when Becky's mother had had a heart attack, she'd dropped everything and moved back home to help care for her. She and Michael had gradually drifted apart, and surprisingly, neither of them seemed to mind much. It was frightening how two people could seem so right for each other, and then grow apart.

C.J. tucked her papers under her arm and strolled toward Grant Park. What a relief to feel brisk morning air after a month of heat and humidity! C.J. noticed that the people on the sidewalks seemed jauntier, more bustling, than they had lately.

Then, with a start, it dawned on her that they all had someplace to go.

She didn't.

For the first time, she missed her old job.

She didn't miss Leonora Nagle, her heinous boss, or Bailey Norwich, the evil production assistant who had been promoted over her, prompting her to quit.

But she did miss a sense of purpose.

Working with Harry had been fun, but it wasn't exactly upwardly mobile. And now it was over. It was time to get serious.

It was August. In another few weeks it would be September—a time that always revved C.J. with that old back-to-school mind-set, a renewed sense of vigor after a long, lazy summer.

If she didn't have a new job by then, what was she going to do? She'd go crazy with boredom . . . not to mention the fact that she'd be destitute. Ever since she'd gotten her last check from Harry, she'd been dipping into her meager savings account every few days—twenty dollars here, fifty there. And David had been more than generous about treating her to meals and movies.

But it was time that she did something about her unemployed state.

Setting her mouth grimly, C.J. crossed Michigan Avenue and entered the park. She plunked herself down on the first bench she came to and opened the first paper to the classified section.

It didn't take long to zero in on, scan and disregard the television production listings. There were only two. One was entry level, and the other was executive level.

Nothing in between.

C.J. let her eyes roam over the other categories of listings, wondering if she really wanted to go back to television after all. There were so many other interesting careers out there. Fashion. Journalism. Publishing.

The only trouble was, she didn't really feel like starting from scratch again. But she didn't feel like going back to a nine-to-five job in television production, either. The position with Harry had been wonderfully unstructured. There were times when she worked around the clock, and other times when she was off for days at a time. It all depended on what Harry's production schedule on his current project was like.

C.J. had discovered that she enjoyed the flexibility. It wasn't going to be easy finding a new job that offered that much freedom. At least, nothing that paid halfway decent.

She sighed and glanced over the classifieds again.

Something caught her eye.

A single word.

Tips.

She zeroed in on that ad, which was for a waitress at a top Chicago restaurant. And that was when she came up with the brilliant idea.

Who said she had to get a "real" job right away? Why couldn't she just get a waitressing job for a while, until she decided what to do next? In fact, she could put off thinking about her career until after the wedding.

Everyone knew waitresses made great tips—at least, some of them did. Didn't they?

And how hard could it be, taking orders and bringing people food? Not nearly as stressful as working in an office had been.

C.J. felt her mouth curving into a smile.

This was a terrific idea.

No need to update her résumé. No need to go out and spend a fortune on business clothes for corporate interviews. No need to hire a pushy headhunter. And no need to worry about a potential employer calling WZZ to check her references.

All she had to do for the time being was land a waitressing job at a place where she could make decent money.

How hard could that be?

"Experience?" the burly-looking man in the dirty white T-shirt barked, looking up at C.J.

"Um...none," she said truthfully. "But I'm a fast learner."

"Honey, I got no time to 'learn' you," he said, creasing her application down the middle, slapping his pudgy hands on top of it and looking at her across the cracked Formica counter. "Sorry."

She hesitated.

"Sorry," he repeated, and stood.

C.J. rose from the stool and shrugged. "It's okay. Thanks for the interview anyway."

He nodded and she walked through the nearly empty diner toward the door. It was no big deal, she told herself. After all, it wasn't as though she'd planned to land a job this quickly.

But when she'd passed Arnie's Diner on her way home from the park and noticed its Waitress Needed sign in the window, she'd thought it couldn't hurt to pop in and inquire. She hadn't expected to have a sauce-stained application shoved in her face, or to be interviewed by Arnie himself immediately upon completing it.

She stepped out onto the sidewalk and continued walking toward home.

Who wants to work in a grungy diner, anyway? she asked herself, still clutching the three newspapers in her hand. *You need to work in a more upscale place to rake in the tips.*

Unfortunately, she also needed experience.

After all, if Arnie didn't have time to train her, how would anyone in a real restaurant agree to?

But it can't be that difficult, C.J. told herself. *After all, we're talking about chatting with customers and carrying trays.*

How hard could that be?

"Experience?" asked the dark-haired woman who was seated across the small round cloth-covered table.

"I spent three years as head waitress at Chez Louis in my hometown," C.J. lied smoothly. The place had closed down last summer when Louis died, and there was no way this woman could prove that C.J. hadn't worked there—was there?

"I see," said the woman, who was the manager of Collette, one of the finest among the cluster of French restaurants in the Loop. They had advertised in *Chicago Now* for "an experienced lunch-shift waitress," and C.J. had been told to come right over when she'd called to ask about it.

"And why did you leave your position at WZZ last year?" the woman asked, patting a nonexistent stray hair into her neat dark bun.

"I decided that I'm not cut out to be a television producer. What I really want to do is be a waitress," she said resolutely.

Which was the truth. For now, at least.

She offered a confident smile.

The woman didn't smile back. "Well, Miss Clarke, I'll be getting back to you soon. I have a few more interviews to conduct before making a decision."

"Oh."

The woman rose.

C.J. did, too.

They shook hands.

"Thank you for coming in," the woman said.

"You're welcome." C.J. followed her to the door. "I'll look forward to hearing from you, then."

"Yes" was all the woman said before C.J. stepped out onto the sidewalk.

She'd been so sure on the way over here that she'd have a job when she left. She'd even thought about how she'd call David from a pay phone and suggest that they meet for lunch so that they could celebrate.

Now it was lunchtime and she was still jobless.

So what? You've only been job hunting for a few hours, she told herself. *What did you expect?*

With a sigh, she headed back toward her apartment.

She might as well spend the afternoon planning her wedding. Those bridal magazines were starting to hold more appeal than job hunting after all.

Two

By Friday, C.J. still hadn't landed a waitress job, but she hadn't lost hope or changed her mind about it. Even David agreed that it was a good idea for her to put off finding a new production job until after the wedding. He had two full weeks of vacation coming, and wanted to take a long honeymoon. C.J. wouldn't be able to do that if she'd just started a new television job.

They hadn't discussed yet exactly *when* they were going to get married, or any other details. Every time one of them had brought it up during the past few days, the other either wasn't in the mood to discuss it, or was falling asleep or was running out the door. So they'd made a date to sit down tonight and talk *wedding*.

C.J. was in the kitchen, chopping vegetables for a stir-fry and waiting for David to show up when someone knocked on the apartment door.

Since visitors had to be buzzed in from the vestibule downstairs, a knock could only mean one thing: it was someone who lived in the building. And since C.J. and Seamus were only friendly with one neighbor, she knew exactly who she'd find standing there when she opened the door.

Christopher McGuire.

"Hey," he said, "what's up?"

"Why don't you tell me?" she asked, doing her best not to look him over from head to toe. But it was so tempting....

Chris was a living, breathing image of C.J.'s "ideal man"—on the outside, at least. Like Dig Lawrence, Chris had dark, dangerous looks, and he tended to dress in faded, ripped jeans and black leather jackets. There had been a time—a *long* time—when C.J. had suffered intensely from unrequited infatuation over Chris. Fortunately, she'd realized that, like Dig Lawrence, Chris had his faults, and that David was really her "ideal man."

Not that he didn't have faults, too—but at least they were faults she could live with.

"Listen to this," Chris said, moving his jean-clad legs apart and tilting his hands vertically in front of him like he was about to reveal something amazing. "We have just been signed by a major label."

"You're kidding!" C.J. knew that *we* was Chris's band.

"I'm *not* kidding. I just got the call a half hour ago. We're on our way—"

"To stardom!" C.J. supplied.

"Hopefully. *And* to New York City. We're leaving Monday."

She frowned. "No."

"Yes."

"For good?"

"It had better be for good. I just called the landlord and gave notice."

C.J. couldn't help feeling wistful. First Becky and Jessica had left. Now Chris would be gone. And in a few months, she'd be moving out, too, when she got married. Everything was changing.

"I'm really psyched for you, Chris," she said, moving forward and giving him a squeeze. "You're really going to make it. Can I say 'I told you so'?"

"Feel free." He grinned at her, rocked backward on his heels and slipped his fingertips into the front pockets of his jeans.

"Told you so."

"Yes, you did. And that's why I wanted you to be one of the first to know."

"Gee, thanks. I feel important. What did Madelyn say?" She was Chris's girlfriend, and once C.J. had gotten past her initial pangs of jealousy, she'd really grown to like her. Quiet, serious Madelyn hadn't seemed like Chris's type, but she was good for him. Somehow she managed to keep him in line. And C.J. suspected he was even more crazy about her than he ever let on.

Chris's smile dimmed. "What could she say? She was happy for me. But she's not exactly thrilled that I'm moving away."

"She's not going with you?"

He shook his head.

"She doesn't want to?"

He paused.

C.J. frowned. "*You* don't want her to."

"It's not that . . . I mean, maybe eventually it'll be a good idea for her to come. But right now, I'm going to be so busy recording, and getting settled in the city and—"

"Chris, if you really wanted her to come, you wouldn't be making excuses like this."

"You're right." He shrugged. "I don't know, C.J. I care about her and everything. . . . I thought things—I thought *I* had changed when Madelyn and I hooked up. But I'm not ready for—you know. For what it would mean if she came to New York with me. Maybe eventually I will be."

"And maybe eventually, she won't be here waiting. Out of sight, out of mind." She knew she shouldn't be standing here, preaching clichés like someone's prune-faced maiden aunt. But somehow she couldn't help it.

"Yeah, well, I'll have to take my chances." Chris looked at her steadily. "Anyway, I just wanted to let you know."

"Chris, don't get me wrong. I'm really, really happy for you. I mean, this is your dream! You're going to be a star."

He nodded and grinned. "Yeah. I really might be."

"I can't believe it. Wait'll I tell David. He's on his way here from work now."

"Work!" Chris snapped his fingers. "That reminds me. I have to call in and tell them I'm going to be late."

"Call in where?"

"Razzles."

"I thought you weren't bartending there anymore."

"I wasn't. But then a few weeks ago, they called and asked me to cover a shift. I was pretty broke and the tips were so great I went back. But now I'm gonna go call them and tell them adios again. For good, I hope."

"Chris, wait a sec. I'm still job hunting. Do you think they'd hire me to take your place?"

He narrowed his eyes at her. "*You* want to be a *bartender?* What happened to C. J. Clarke, up and coming television exec?"

"I've decided not to go back into the rat race until after David and I get married. I just need to make some money between now and then."

"Well, you'll definitely make some bucks at Razzles. Especially on margarita night. People drink two of those, and they start getting reckless, tipping you fives and tens to get your attention cause the bar's so jammed."

"Think I could make a hundred a night?"

"Easy. Twice that on a good night."

Ch-ching—C.J. heard an imaginary cash register in her head. That was almost as much as she'd made in a *week* as a lowly production assistant at WZZ, or working for Harry. "Are you serious?"

"Would I lie about money? Listen, I've got to go call Marty. Want me to tell him I've got a replacement?"

"Definitely. But won't he want to interview me?"

"Nah. Probably not. He's not really into formal management. Do you have any experience?"

"Uh—as a bartender?"

"I didn't think so," he said, studying her. "I've got to work tonight and tomorrow. Weekends are always hopping, and I could use the extra cash before I leave. But listen, you help me pack boxes on Sunday afternoon, and I'll give you a crash course in mixology. Okay?''

"Deal." She took a deep breath and let it out. "I can't believe I'm actually going to be a bartender. Are you sure Marty will be into hiring me?''

"Why not?" Chris shrugged and edged out the door. "I've got to run."

"Okay. Call and let me know what he says."

"I will."

Chris headed back over to his apartment.

Five minutes later, as C.J. was measuring a tiny trickle of sesame oil into her wok, the phone rang.

It was Chris.

"Well?" she asked, balancing the phone between her head and shoulder as she spread the oil over the hot surface with a wooden spatula.

"Congratulations. You got yourself a bartending job."

"You got yourself a *what?*" David asked, his fork poised midway between his plate and mouth.

"A bartending job," C.J. said. "At Razzles. I start on Tuesday night."

David lowered his fork and put it down, letting the chicken, rice and vegetables spill off it. "You're going to be a bartender."

"Yes."

"My fiancée is going to be a bartender."

C.J. felt a little twinge of anger. "That's right," she said resolutely, putting down her own fork.

David hesitated, and she could see the wheels working in his mind. For a moment, she thought he was going to yell at her, but he didn't. His voice was calm, as usual, when he finally spoke. But she knew him well enough to sense the tension in his tone. "C.J., I don't like this one bit."

"What do you mean? You liked it just fine the other day when I explained that I could make a lot of money in tips if I got a job at a restaurant."

"You were talking about waitressing. This is different."

"Yeah. The tips are even better." She reached for her glass and took a sip of wine. Suddenly she wished she hadn't set the table with candles and flowers and made such a big deal about dinner. She'd wanted to celebrate her new job. Obviously, David didn't.

He clamped his mouth shut, looked off into the distance for a long moment and then met her gaze again. "I'm worried about you, that's all."

"Why? You know what Razzles is like. I mean, for heaven's sake, David, *we* hang out there."

"I know, but it's different to think of you working there. In a bar."

"Razzles is a restaurant."

"A bar-restaurant. At night, it's a pick-up place."

He had a point. Razzles was where C.J.'s fateful encounter with Dig Lawrence had been launched.

She fought back a twinge of guilt about that and said, "So what? I'm going to be working there, not sitting at the bar in a miniskirt wearing a come-hither look."

Not that the sight of her in a miniskirt would make the opposite sex come hither. Run in the opposite direction was more like it.

"Things happen in bars," David said evenly. "There are drugs. There are drunks. There are fights. It's not the kind of atmosphere a woman should be working in, C.J. And besides—"

Just then, as C.J. was preparing to cut in and attack David for being a chauvinist, the intercom buzzed.

David broke off midsentence and looked at her. "Are you expecting someone?"

"No. And Seamus is out with Chad." She shrugged. "I'll go see who it is."

She got up and walked over to the intercom panel next to the door. "Yes?" she asked, holding the talk button down.

"Surprise!"

C.J. winced at the blast and frowned. She looked over her shoulder at David, who had followed her into the hall.

"Who was that?"

"I have no idea." She pushed the talk button again and said, "Um, excuse me? I think you have the wrong apartment."

The only response was another "Surprise!"

"That sounded like..." David said.

"I know who it sounded like," she snapped. "But it can't be."

Please, God, don't let it be.

She pressed the talk button again. "Who is this?" she asked, trying to keep her voice calm.

"Clara Joy, it's your mother," came the booming reply.

"And me, too!"

"Oh my God. That's Fawn," David said, turning pale beneath his ruddy summer complexion. "What's *she* doing here?"

"What's my mother doing here?"

Before C.J. could react, she heard Lila say, "For goodness' sake, Clara Joy, will you buzz us in?"

Like an automaton, C.J. depressed the door button.

She and David looked at each other.

"What the hell are they *doing* here? Did you know about this, C.J.?"

"Oh, please, David. Do you think I would have stayed in town if I had?"

This was just like her mother. She'd always threatened to "drop by" unexpectedly. And now that C.J. was engaged to marry Lila's old sorority sister's stepson, she probably thought it would be even more fun if Fawn came along, too.

C.J. tried to grasp the fact that Fawn had obviously flown in from Western New York, where she lived with David's father. Why on earth hadn't she told David she was coming? Why hadn't Lila told C.J.?

David opened the apartment door and looked out into the hallway. "The elevator just dinged," he told C.J., trepidation mounting on his face.

And for good reason.

Within moments, Lila Clarke and Fawn Mallomack Griffin were descending upon them.

"Mom...I can't believe this," C.J. said weakly as her mother grabbed her and squeezed her.

"We thought we'd surprise you two," Lila said, grabbing David as C.J.'s future stepmother-in-law hugged her next.

"We're having a girls' weekend in Chicago. I convinced Lila she had to get away, after all she's been through with Kyle these past few months," Fawn said, releasing C.J. and glancing around the apartment. "Oh, this is charming."

"Girls' weekend?" David echoed, as C.J. mumbled, "Thanks."

The two women breezed in, enveloping the place in a cloud of spicy perfume.

C.J. and David followed, exchanging a panic-stricken glance.

"Oh my goodness, Lila. Look! We're interrupting their romantic little candlelight dinner," Fawn said, stopping short when she caught sight of the table.

"It's okay," David said.

C.J. shot him a narrow look.

"I mean," he went on, "we were almost finished. So, what a surprise."

"I knew it would be," Lila said gleefully. "Remember when I called you this morning, Clara Joy, and asked what you had planned for tonight? I was so glad you said you'd be home. I'll bet you never guessed I had a little trick up my sleeve."

"No. No, I sure didn't," C.J. said numbly.

"I took the four o'clock flight in from Buffalo, and Lila picked me up at the airport," Fawn told them. "We stopped at the Hyatt to check in, then came straight here."

The Hyatt. They were staying at the Hyatt, not here.

Thankful for that small blessing, C.J. said, "Would you like something to drink? Wine, or—"

"I'd love a glass of wine," Fawn told her. "Lila?"

"Sounds wonderful." C.J.'s mother was examining a framed photo. "Who are these two young men, Clara Joy?"

"That's Seamus, my roommate. And that's his, uh, *friend.* His name's Chad."

"Oh, of course. Seamus is a homosexual," Lila informed Fawn.

C.J. knew her mother liked to think that she was "hip," as she often put it.

Fawn's eyebrows went up. "Really?"

"Uh, why don't you both have a seat?" David asked, taking the photo out of Lila's hands and guiding the two women to the couch.

C.J. hurriedly poured two glasses of wine and brought them over. Then she went back to the table for her own glass, and David's. She drained hers in a long gulp, refilled it, then joined the others.

"So, what brings you two to Chicago?" she asked, feeling a little wobbly as the wine warmed its way down her insides. She perched on the edge of a chair and looked first at her mother, then at Fawn.

"Remember, C.J.?" David asked dryly. "Girls' weekend."

"Oh, right. So, are you going to see a show or something?"

"Well, actually, Clara Joy, what we really wanted to see was you. And David. The soon-to-be bride and groom. If it hadn't been for Kyle's accident, we would have done this months ago. But now that your brother's much better and will be back to college soon for the fall semester, well, we're here to make wedding plans," Lila said.

C.J. had been about to sip her wine. It turned into a gulp that burned her throat. "Uh . . . wedding plans?"

"That's right," Fawn said happily. "You two haven't even set a date yet. It was very noble of you to put it off in light of Kyle's, um, *tragedy.* But at this rate, by the time you actually tie the knot, you'll be too old to give us grandchildren!"

"Grandchildren?" C.J. echoed. She looked at David.

"Well, it was really nice of the two of you to come all this way to help us plan our wedding," he said. "But actually, we've been making plans on our own."

"You have?" Lila looked surprised.

"Sure," C.J. lied. "We've decided exactly what kind of ceremony and reception we want. Haven't we, David?"

"Yup. We have."

"Well, we can't wait to hear all about it. Can we, Lila?" Fawn asked.

"No. No, we certainly can't."

C.J. caught the glance that passed between the two women. A glance that said, *No matter what these two think they want, we'll talk them out of it.*

She cleared her throat. "Well, for a start, we don't want anything big or fancy. Just a small, simple wedding."

"That's right," David said. "We don't want some big black-tie affair."

C.J. shot him a grateful look.

"But," Lila quickly inserted, "Clara Joy, you know our family isn't small. Why, with aunts, uncles and cousins, there are easily dozens of people."

"Well, Mom, we'll just have to limit the guest list."

"But—"

"Don't worry, Lila, I'm sure we'll be able to work out the details," David said, shooting a warning look at C.J. "We don't want to leave anyone out."

"What church did you have in mind?" Fawn asked, gracefully setting her wineglass down on the table.

"Church?" David echoed. "Oh, well, we aren't certain that our wedding will be in a church."

We aren't? C.J. wondered. Had David come around to her way of thinking? Maybe she'd somehow convinced him that barefoot on the beach was really the way to go.

"After all," David continued, "I'm Jewish. I wouldn't feel comfortable getting married in the church."

Startled, C.J. looked at him. She had never even considered that he might not want to get married in a Catholic ceremony in church.

Lila looked stricken. "David, I realize that your late mother was Jewish, and that you technically are, too, but I assumed you weren't religious."

C.J. jumped in quickly. "Mom, he never said that."

Actually, he had—to her. And she'd never suspected that he might want a Jewish wedding. She didn't even know how she felt about it. Her mind was suddenly whirling.

"David, your sisters were married in the church," Fawn said pointedly. "Remember?"

"Roxie wasn't."

"Lauren *was.*"

"But that doesn't mean I want to be."

Way to go, David! C.J. thought, reaching over and giving his arm a squeeze. It was so unlike him to make waves. But then again, this was the first time she'd ever seen him interacting with his stepmother. There was an ornery gleam in David's eye that C.J. had never glimpsed before.

"In fact, I'm hoping that we can find a rabbi who's willing to co-officiate with a priest on neutral territory," David concluded, glancing at C.J.

She was so surprised, all she could do was nod.

A rabbi and a priest?

Lila looked more than a little taken aback. "But, Clara Joy, I had assumed that you'd be married in our hometown church, with Father Manelli doing the ceremony."

She found her voice. "Mom, I never said that."

"But you never said you *wouldn't* get married in the church. For heaven's sake—what about Grandma?"

"What about her?"

"She's going to be upset if you don't have a church wedding."

"No, she won't," C.J. said firmly, despite her own uncertainty.

Her mother's mother *was* pretty religious. And before he'd died a few years ago, Grandpa Tony had gone to Mass every day. Her father's parents, who had both died when she was in junior high, had also been devout Catholics.

There was an awkward pause. They all just looked at each other.

Finally Fawn asked, "What month did you have in mind for the wedding?"

"Well, we want to be married before the end of the year," David said.

"A winter wedding?" Lila looked dubious. "But the weather here is always so unpredictable."

"We don't mind. That way, no one will be expecting a beautiful sunny day, and no one will be disappointed when it's not."

"But, David, your father and I—and the rest of your family—will have to fly in from Buffalo," Fawn said. "Lord knows, a blizzard can blow in and close the airport at a moment's notice."

"Well, we'll just have to take our chances. I don't want to wait any longer to get married. C.J. and I are anxious to start our new life. Aren't we, C.J.?"

"We sure are," she said, smiling at him.

But all she could think was that she hoped weddings weren't an indication of how marriages turned out—because theirs was bound to be a full-scale disaster.

David walked back into the apartment looking shell-shocked.

C.J. looked up from the sink, where she was washing the four wineglasses. "Did you get them safely into a cab?"

"Uh-huh." He came up behind her, slipped his arms around her, and kissed the back of her neck. "Thank you."

"For what?" She stopped sloshing the sponge in a glass and leaned against him.

"For not strangling your mother and Fawn the moment they announced that they were here to plan our wedding."

"In that case, thank *you* for not doing it, either. Can you believe them?"

David released her and stepped over to the refrigerator. He opened it, took out a beer and popped off the top. "Want one?"

"Nah," C.J. said. "You know what they say about mixing the grape and the grain."

"Right now, anything would be better than dealing with those two again tomorrow. Even a monster hangover."

"You're right. I'll have one, too." C.J. rinsed the last glass and put it onto the rack to dry.

David handed her his open beer, got another one for himself and sat down at the table. C.J. leaned against the counter and took a long swallow.

They looked at each other.

"They're going to drive us crazy before this is over," David commented bleakly. *"Crazy."*

"I know."

"What are we going to do?"

C.J. shrugged. She walked over and sat down next to him. "I didn't know you wanted an interfaith ceremony."

"I didn't, either, until I said it. But the way Fawn breezed in here and started making plans, as though *she* were my mother..." He shook his head.

"I know," C.J. said, reaching over and squeezing his hand. David rarely talked about his real mother, who had died of cancer when he was in his teens.

"Does it bother you?"

"Does what bother me?" she asked, knowing exactly what he was talking about and not wanting to reply because she had no idea what she wanted to say.

"An interfaith wedding."

She hesitated.

David was watching her carefully.

"I don't know," she said honestly.

"You wouldn't feel comfortable with a rabbi there?"

"It's not that. I mean, it just seems like if we make that much of a point to have a religious ceremony, it wouldn't be honest or real."

"What's that supposed to mean? It wouldn't be 'real'? Real, how?"

It wasn't exactly as if he was *angry*. But he still had that unfamiliar look in his eye, and C.J. got the feeling that they were treading on dangerous ground here. Which was ridiculous, because religion had just never been a big deal between them.

"David, all I mean is, wouldn't having a big production involving a priest and a rabbi be even more religious than just having a simple church wedding?"

"Or a simple synagogue wedding?"

"A synagogue?" She hadn't thought of that. Would she be comfortable getting married in a synagogue? She wanted to think that yes, of course she would be. But the truth was, she knew she wouldn't be.

Why did this have to be so complicated all of a sudden? "What I'm saying, David, is that maybe we should just have a simple civil ceremony. We can get a justice of the peace, and—why are you making that face?"

"Because. A justice of the peace would be impersonal. If we were going to go that route, we might as well just go down to city hall tomorrow and get hitched."

Now C.J. was the one making the face.

"What's the matter?" David asked. "Wasn't it just the other day that you were telling me you wanted an unconventional wedding?"

"Yes, but I didn't mean a five-minute city hall deal." *And I didn't mean a rabbi and a priest, either,* she added silently.

"What did you mean?" David asked. "Wait, don't answer that. I know what you meant. Barefoot on the beach, right?"

"David—"

"C.J. . . ." He shook his head.

She sipped her beer and looked at him.

He sipped his beer and looked back at her.

"How would we even find both a priest and a rabbi who would be willing to do this?" she asked.

"I'm not sure," he admitted. "According to what I've heard, it's not exactly a piece of cake."

"Have you ever been to a wedding like that? An interfaith ceremony, I mean?"

"No."

"What did your sisters do?"

"Roxie got married in a civil ceremony on a military base where Lou was stationed. And Lauren and Andy were married in a Catholic church. Andy's brother is a priest."

"Oh." C.J. thought about how David had always said he and his sister Lauren were a lot alike. Obviously, not that much alike, since David had told Fawn that even though his sister had done it, he wouldn't feel comfortable getting married in a church.

They sipped their beers again.

C.J. sighed. Why was their wedding suddenly feeling like something to dread, rather than something to look forward to?

"Did you hear what my mother said about finding an orchestra?" she asked David.

"Yes. I had something a little less...*huge* in mind. Maybe a regular old band."

"Or an alternative band—or even a deejay. But I didn't even want to bring it up. I mean, David—an orchestra? What are they going to play? 'Stardust'? Our friends won't be into that. And besides, an orchestra is going to cost a fortune."

"Our parents don't mind, apparently. And since they're paying..."

Lila and Fawn had repeatedly assured C.J. and David that money was no object. The two families were going to be splitting the cost of the wedding, and they wanted it to be, as Fawn kept putting it, "an affair to remember."

Whenever she used that particular phrase, C.J. thought of the tragic old movie by that name, and how the heroine had been mowed down by a cab on her way to meet the hero, and how it had ripped their romance apart. C.J. had sobbed through the entire film. Mentally linking it to her wedding wasn't a good omen. Leave it to Fawn to keep bringing it up.

And every time C.J. and David protested that they didn't want anything huge and elaborate, both Fawn and Lila hastily assured them that that wasn't what they had in mind. Then they'd resumed their chatter about caterers, floral arrangements and parking attendants.

"Maybe *we* should pay for the whole thing," C.J. suggested now, peeling the corner of the silver foil label on her beer bottle. "Then we won't have to let them have any say in the plans."

"We could...but do you know how much weddings cost?"

"You're right. There's no way." C.J. took another swallow of her beer and yawned.

"Tired?" David asked.

"Yes."

"Me, too. Let's go to bed. Before we know it, we'll have to meet our two self-appointed wedding planners for that breakfast at the Hyatt. I can't believe they insisted on eight o'clock."

"I know, but there's no arguing with them." C.J. stood and poured the remaining beer in her bottle down the drain as David tilted his head and polished his off.

She was too tired to talk about the wedding anymore. They could worry about it later. Maybe after she'd given it some thought, she'd have a better idea of how she felt about an interfaith ceremony. Right now, her mind was a total blur.

"Ready?" David asked, putting his empty bottle on the counter next to hers.

"Yes. But, David? Before we go to bed, I want to tell you one thing."

"What?"

"It kind of got lost in the shuffle after my mother and Fawn showed up. But that bartending job? I'm taking it, David."

He gave her a long look. "C.J.—"

"David, this is *my* decision. I want to do it."

He shook his head, but didn't say anything.

"Look, David, there are going to be times when you don't agree with things I want to do, and vice versa—before and after we're married. That doesn't mean we get to give each other orders. If I want to work in a bar for a while, that's my decision."

"But I'm going to be worried about you, especially knowing that you'll be coming home in the middle of the night by yourself and—"

"David, I'll be *fine*," she cut in. "And you can't stop me by trying to make me scared. I'm going to do this."

He set his mouth and shrugged.

"Don't be mad."

He didn't say anything.

"Come on, David." She put her hand on his sleeve. "Can we kiss and make up?"

For a moment, he just looked at her. Then he leaned over and gave her a kiss. It started out as a brief peck and somehow turned into something more passionate.

How had that happened? How had irritation segued right into attraction?

C.J. was still annoyed with him, and she could tell he felt the same way. But there was something undeniably sexy about this new side of David she'd witnessed tonight—a stubborn, almost confrontational side of him. He suddenly didn't seem quite like familiar, sensible David, and it turned her on.

C.J. wrapped her arms around his neck and pressed against him. "I'm not as tired as I thought I was," she whispered, and moved her lips over the smooth skin below his ear.

"Me, either," he said, and gave a little moan as she moved down to the hollow above his collarbone. "But let's go to bed anyway."

"Mom, I told you, I really don't want to go shopping for a wedding dress," C.J. said desperately as the taxi neared their destination.

"Clara Joy, you can't put this off until the last minute. Especially if you're going to be getting married in December. It takes months for alterations to be made, and you'll need to have fittings, and more fittings—it'll be wonderful. You'll see. Oh, cabbie, that's it ahead. On the right."

C.J. cringed, and not just because Lila had called the driver "cabbie." When she glanced in the direction her mother was pointing, she saw the enormous sign that marked the site of Weissman's Wedding Warehouse.

Yikes.

Her mother had insisted that somewhere on those three floors, C.J.'s dream dress was waiting.

Yeah, right.

She sighed and climbed out of the cab as her mother paid the driver. This was going to be horrible.

Lucky David. He'd gotten off easily. He and Fawn were going to lunch and a matinee.

He'd acted like that was a horrible fate until C.J. reminded him what an ordeal shopping for clothes with her mother had always been. Trying to pick out a wedding dress would be pure torture. Lila had a way of dishing out back-handed compliments when they shopped—gems like, "Oh, look, Clara Joy, that dress would look wonderful on you. That drop waist will probably take off ten pounds. Fifteen, if you get it in a dark color."

Now, as C.J. and Lila made their way through the crowd of women in the warehouse entrance, she prayed for strength. Her mother was going to demand that she try on one gown after another. She just knew it.

Sure enough. "Oh, look at that, Clara Joy," Lila said, stopping just inside the door to point at a mannequin wearing an elaborate gown. "Isn't that just precious? Why don't you try that on for a start?"

"Nah," C.J. said, trying to regain her footing as a group of giggling, eager girls, none of them a day over eighteen, jostled her on their way to inspect a sales rack.

"'Nah'?" Lila echoed, and pursed her burgundy-lipsticked lips.

"Mom, it's not my style. I want something plain. You know, a dress. Not a gown."

Her mother just looked at her. "A dress? This is your wedding, Clara Joy. You need to wear a wedding *gown*."

"What's wrong with a wedding *dress?*"

"I'm afraid I don't understand your point," Lila said, clutching her purse tightly as another wave of wedding-crazed women engulfed them. "Wedding dress, wedding gown—it's the same thing."

"No, it's not, Mom. I don't want to look like the top of a wedding cake, dripping in ruffles and rosettes. I want to be simple. Plain. *Me.*"

Her mother frowned. "Clara Joy, this is the one day in your life when you're expected to shine. You can't show up in a plain old white dress."

"Who said white?"

The look of horror that came over Lila's face was so pure that C.J. quickly said, "Don't worry, Mom. I'll find something to wear. Maybe even something white. I just don't think I'm going to find it in this place.''

Her mother sighed. "Clara Joy, will you do one thing to humor me?''

"What?''

"Just look? That's all I'm asking. I'm not going to force you into a dressing room with a gaudy gown, for heaven's sake. All I'm asking is that you simply look around and get some ideas. Okay?''

C.J. thought it over, then nodded. "Fine. We'll just look.''

A dozen gaudy gowns later, C.J. was mentally kicking herself.

She should have known that her mother would manage to wheedle her into trying things on—"just for ideas, of course.''

She was forced, repeatedly, to stand fat and seminaked in her cotton underwear and big white bra, while the attendant, a woman who introduced herself as Miss Marge, and her mother—both of whom insisted on coming in with her every time—struggled to undo buttons, zippers and eye hooks on the gowns. She'd loathed every single gown that was eventually pulled over her head, and she'd hated the way her mother would insist that Miss Marge "keep trying" to fasten C.J. into gowns that were obviously too small.

And whenever C.J. was certain that the ordeal was finally over, Miss Marge would say, "I *do* have one more frock—'' she called all the gowns frocks "—that might be just what you're looking for." And then she'd vanish, and reappear with another hideous white balloon of fabric.

At least Lila didn't try to talk C.J. into buying any of the gowns she tried on. How could she? No one in their right mind would find the ghastly contraptions flattering. They all transformed C.J.'s hips and behind into overstuffed pillows and her bust into a formidable wall of cleavage that wasn't sexy so much as it was *scary*.

Finally, mercifully, Miss Marge had exhausted all of her frocks.

She was obviously at a loss when Lila said simply, "Thank you. I believe we'll just browse on our own for a while."

"But..." Miss Marge feebly began a token protest.

"We're finished. Thanks anyway," C.J. told her.

She and Lila made their way out of the labyrinth of dressing rooms, back onto the warehouse floor.

"Why don't we look over there?" Lila asked brightly, gesturing to a far-off corner.

"Mom, I've had enough for today," C.J. said. "I really don't think this place has what I'm looking for. But thanks anyway," she added quickly, cutting off her mother's attempt to dissuade her.

Wordlessly, they shouldered their way through the frenzied shoppers until they were back out on the street. C.J. scanned the busy avenue for a cab.

Luckily, one pulled up within seconds, depositing a pretty, slender blonde and an attractive older woman onto the sidewalk.

C.J. and Lila slid into the back seat. Just before the cab pulled out into traffic, C.J. heard the younger woman say to the other, "I can't wait to try on gowns, Mom. This is going to be so much fun!"

C.J. turned her head and watched the mother and daughter disappear into the warehouse together as the cab headed down the street.

On the seat beside her, Lila was also glancing back at them.

After a moment, they both faced forward again.

Then Lila said, "Oh, Clara Joy, I really wanted to help you pick out your wedding gown. I've only got one daughter, you know. And this is something a mother dreams about her whole life."

C.J. found herself softening. "I know, Mom. But I just can't help it. Those 'frocks' aren't my style. And besides— I'm not ready to get a dress yet."

"But if you and David want to be married before the end of the year, the wedding is only—"

"A few months away. I know. But I'm going to put off shopping for a dress anyway."

"Why?"

C.J. just shrugged and looked out the window at the traffic. She wasn't about to tell her mother that she planned to go on a diet, starting tomorrow. A *real* diet and exercise program, for the first time in her life.

Damned if she'd be caught dead in public wearing one of Miss Marge's frocks.

But she was going to be a thin bride if it killed her.

C.J. thought about the idea of an interfaith wedding all during dinner Saturday night. And long after David had fallen asleep when they got back to her apartment, she lay there in the dark, wondering what to do.

She couldn't help wondering why it suddenly seemed so important to David that they have a religious ceremony with a rabbi involved. It wasn't that his Jewish faith bothered C.J. And it wasn't necessarily the idea of going out of their way to have a religious ceremony when she personally wasn't religious.

No, what was *really* bothering her, when it came right down to it, was that she didn't understand where this whole angle was coming from. David, predictable David, the person she had thought she knew inside and out, had sprung this idea on her out of the blue, and that was troubling.

David had admitted to not being religious. In fact, he was so *non*religious that C.J. hadn't even known he was Jewish until it came up incidentally last year. And even then, he had shrugged it off.

Now, suddenly, he was bent on having an interfaith ceremony. Why? How could she not have known this about him? How could it have caught her off guard? Where was he coming from?

She poked him in the shoulder blades until he woke up.

"What is it?" he asked groggily. "What's wrong?"

"I was just wondering if we could talk about the wedding for a minute."

He groaned and rolled over onto his back. *"Now?"*

"David, I just need to know why this is so important to you."

"The wedding?"

"Having a rabbi there."

He was silent for a moment. Then he said, "It just is."

She sensed that it would be useless to push him further—that he wasn't going to go into it. That was all there was to it.

Mentally, C.J. sighed. She was so weary of the whole wedding thing already, and they hadn't even *really* begun to make plans yet. How was she going to survive the next few months?

Impulsively, she reached out and put her arm across David's chest, letting her fingertips rest against his heart. The soft fabric of his T-shirt and the rhythmic beating of his heart were reassuring.

"David?" she whispered in the dark.

"Yeah?" he whispered back.

"Let's see what we can do. About the rabbi and the priest, I mean. If it's that important to you, I think we should go for it."

He pulled her closer, and brushed his lips against her hair, and she knew that what she'd just said mattered a great deal to him.

She just wished she knew why.

Three

"This is going to be awful," C.J. said, casting a nervous glance at David as he pulled the car to a stop in front of the split-level home in suburban Oak Hills where she'd grown up.

He shut off the engine. "Stop saying that."

"Stop saying, 'Stop saying that'! Trust me, this weekend is going to be awful. I've been dreading it all week."

David looked at her. "I don't know what your problem is," he said, sounding irritated.

Even-tempered David was rarely irritated.

It must be the humidity. And the three-hour drive.

The Friday-night traffic out of Chicago had been horrendous. It was usually pretty bad, but this was Labor Day weekend. And the temperature was in the high nineties even now that the sun had set.

It didn't help that C.J. and David had spent the first hour of the trip arguing about the air conditioner. David had stubbornly refused to turn it on since they were sitting still in bumper-to-bumper traffic. C.J. had sat there, sweating and fuming, as they inched their way out of the city.

And as soon as they'd made it out onto the open road and turned on the air conditioner at last, their argument had shifted focus. C.J. had complained about coming home to plan the wedding this weekend, while David the pacifist tried to calm her down. His unruffled attitude had only made her grumpier.

"You can't put this off indefinitely, C.J.," David reminded her again now. "We have to meet with Father Maloney—"

"Manelli," she corrected crankily.

"Manelli. And we have to look at those places your mother has picked out for the wedding so that we can set the date."

"David, I'll tell you right now that Father Manelli isn't going to be thrilled about my getting married in a half-Jewish ceremony outside the church. I don't know why you talked me into listening to my mother and meeting with him at all."

"Because it can't hurt, that's why. You never know. Maybe he'll help us."

"You don't know Father Manelli. I mean, he makes the Pope seem liberal. And anyway, I don't even *want* to get married out here in the suburbs. I wanted our wedding to be in Chicago. We can find some loft space right in the Loop and make it look terrific."

"Yeah, well, since we're not paying for the wedding, C.J., I think we'd better go along with whatever your mother has in mind. Anyway, it'll be nicer out here. This is where you grew up. This is where your family is, and all your old friends."

C.J. sighed. "This weekend is going to be a nightmare. I just know it" was all she said.

David put his hand on the door handle and looked at her. "Are we going to go in? Or are we going to sit here in the car all night?"

"You think I'm being a baby, don't you?"

"I didn't say that."

"You were thinking it. And you're right." She wiped sweat from under her hairline along her forehead. "I guess we better go in. It's too sweltering to sit in the car without air-conditioning. This is like being back on the expressway." She opened the door and climbed out.

The cul de sac was pretty quiet, as usual. Crickets chirped and, down the street in the Gearys' backyard, she could hear children splashing in a pool.

C.J. walked around to the trunk of the car. David opened it and shouldered their two overnight bags.

"I'll take this," she said, tugging on the strap of her own bag.

"I've got it. Just shut the trunk."

"David, don't be silly. You don't have to carry both bags. Let me take one."

"C.J., if you don't stop pulling on the strap, this is going to fall. I've got it." He started up the driveway toward the house.

C.J. shrugged, slammed the trunk and followed.

She and David walked past a familiar compact car with a University of Illinois/Urbana-Champaign sticker in the back window. Good. Kyle was here already. Having him around always helped to divert her mother's attention from C.J.

Lila worshiped her son. Somehow, despite his doting mother, he hadn't turned into the spoiled brat C.J. had always expected him to become. As Lila relentlessly pointed out, Kyle had it all—great looks, athletic prowess, good grades. And somehow, none of it had gone to his head.

He'd already just started the fall semester, but had driven back here for the long weekend. C.J.'s mother had called her earlier this week and reported that Kyle and Tammy had broken up. Lila was disgusted with Tammy, wondering how on earth she could leave Kyle "in his time of need."

But C.J. knew it was more complicated than that. Kyle had been driving the van the night of the accident, and Tammy's sorority sister, Maggie, had been killed. C.J. knew her brother had a lot of grief and guilt over it, and it had obviously put a strain on his relationship with Tammy. And even though it had been obvious they really cared about each other, C.J. had always suspected it was only a matter of time before Tammy moved on.

After all, she was older than Kyle. She had graduated in June and wasn't going to hang around a college town forever. Kyle still had two more years of school left.

C.J. knew her brother had always been able to bounce back easily, but this time she was worried about him.

She and David walked up the back steps to the wooden deck, then over to the sliding glass doors that opened off the kitchen.

There, sitting around the table, were her parents and Kyle. C.J. knocked on the glass.

Her father came over and unlocked the door. "You're here. We were just getting worried about you two." He gave her a big squeeze, then shook David's hand. "Was traffic bad?"

"Pretty bad," David said.

C.J. sighed in relief as she stepped into the wonderfully air-conditioned kitchen.

Lila hummed "Here Comes the Bride" as she stood and hugged C.J.

"Hi, Mom," she said around clenched teeth.

Her mother stopped humming, stepped back, looked at her and tilted her head.

C.J. knew Lila was checking to see if she'd lost any weight. She hadn't. If anything, she'd gained a few pounds this week. Stress always made her extra hungry, and she'd been a basket case just thinking about this weekend.

She looked past her mother. Kyle was sitting at the table, looking uncharacteristically glum. C.J. forced a light note into her voice and said, "Hey, look at you, Blondie."

"My hair always gets lighter in the summer" was all he said.

"Especially when you put lemon juice in it," C.J. teased him. She'd caught him doing just that a few summers ago and had vowed never to let him live it down.

Kyle just smiled briefly. C.J. noticed the shadows beneath his beautiful green eyes.

"How are you feeling?" David asked. "All healed?"

Kyle shrugged. "I guess."

"Good."

C.J. and her mother exchanged a look. For once, they were on the same wavelength. C.J. was thinking that her brother may have been healed on the outside, but inside, he was still torn up, and he would be for a long time.

"My goodness, look at how that ring of yours is sparkling, Clara Joy," her mother said after an uncomfortable pause.

C.J. looked down at the pear-shaped diamond in its simple gold setting. When David had first given it to her, she'd been constantly conscious of its presence. Every time she'd moved her hand during those initial few weeks, the unfamiliar glint had startled her. But she'd almost gotten used to it over the past year.

Now she admired it again, and felt instantly better about everything.

David went to put the luggage in the bedrooms down the hall, and C.J. went over to the refrigerator and took out a bottle of Snapple Diet Iced Tea. She poured some into a glass, drank it down and refilled it. "I'm totally dehydrated. Why is it so hot out? It's September. It's supposed to cool off."

"Don't change the subject, Clara Joy," Lila said. "We're all anxious to talk about the wedding."

Oh, great. C.J. put her glass on the counter and ran a hand through her long, spiral-curled hair. "What's to talk about? We haven't even set the date yet."

"Well, that's why you're here," Lila told her. "After you talk to Father Manelli tomorrow, we'll go look at the places Daddy and I have picked out for the reception."

"*And* ceremony," C.J. said. "Don't forget that we're going to be married wherever we're having the reception."

Her mother's smile faded. "Yes, well, after you talk to Father Manelli—"

"Mom," C.J. interrupted, "you *know* we're not getting married in the church, right? I hope you told Father Manelli that when you set up this appointment for us."

Her mother hesitated.

"Dad?" C.J. asked, looking at him. "What did she tell him?"

"Don't worry, C.J." Her father took a long drink of whatever was in his glass and set it down. "No one expects you to get married in a church."

"Good." C.J. glanced at her mother again.

Lila said, "Clara Joy, I was talking to my friend Sarah Stein the other day, and she said it's nearly impossible to find a rabbi who'd be willing to perform an interfaith ceremony...."

An unsuspecting David came back into the room. *Look out, David,* C.J. warned mentally.

"Isn't that right, David?" Lila tacked on smoothly.

"Isn't what right?"

"She said that she heard it's impossible to find a rabbi to do an interfaith ceremony," C.J. said, and turned back to her mother. "There were three types of rabbis. Orthodox, Conservative and Reform. The first two won't support an interfaith marriage. Reform will."

"Might," David corrected.

"Might," C.J. agreed.

"But we should be able to find someone," David said with his trademark unruffled optimism.

C.J. saw her parents exchanging a glance. She read her mother's expression: *Hopefully they won't find a willing rabbi.*

Her father's said, *Stay out of this, Lila.*

"So," C.J. said brightly, after a pause. "I started my new job."

"What new job?" Kyle asked.

"Jeez, doesn't Mom give anybody any news about me? I'm a bartender at Razzles."

Her parents exchanged another glance.

"You're a *bartender?*" Kyle asked.

"Yeah," C.J. said, conscious of David's stiff posture beside her.

He still wasn't happy about the whole thing, even though C.J. had been working at Razzles for over a week now. The first few nights she'd been there, until she'd put a stop to it, he'd showed up at the bar just before closing and insisted on driving her home. Now she took cabs, and when he wasn't waiting up for her at her place, he called to make sure she'd arrived safely.

She chattered brightly for a few minutes about how much fun it was to work at Razzles and to have a job she could leave behind, mentally, when her shift was over.

C.J.'s parents' faces were no more enthusiastic than David's. Obviously, they weren't thrilled about having their daughter work as a bartender. Kyle, who in the past could have been counted on for support, sat there absently fiddling with the straw place mat in front of him.

"I made a hundred and fifty dollars in tips last night alone," C.J. said. "And they're really good about giving me time off whenever I need it. They didn't blink an eye when I told them I was going away this weekend."

"But, Clara Joy, a bartender? It's so—"

"C.J. won't be working at Razzles forever," David interrupted pointedly. "She's going back to her production career after the honeymoon. Right, C.J.?"

"Right," she said, although she wasn't so sure she wanted to be a television producer anymore. Working a mindless job like bartending was so liberating...less stress, more money. But she could just imagine what David and her parents would think if she told them she wanted to make bartending a permanent career. Not that she wanted to do *that,* but...she didn't know what she wanted.

"Are you hungry, David?" Lila asked abruptly, standing. "There's leftover Kentucky Fried Chicken in the fridge. We had it for dinner. It was too hot to cook. I think there's a whole container of mashed potatoes there, and some biscuits, too. And I have lettuce and tomatoes in the crisper for a salad," she added, for C.J.'s benefit.

C.J. sighed inwardly. Her mother would never suggest that *she* eat fried chicken. All her life, Lila had been doing her best to guide her toward skim milk and carrot sticks while peddling cookies, potato chips and other good stuff to everyone else.

Someday, C.J. vowed, she'd be so thin that her mother would take one look at her and say, "Oh, my goodness, Clara Joy, you'd better get some meat on those bones."

Not *someday*.

Her wedding day.

She willed her mouth to stop watering as her mother took a familiar red-and-white cardboard bucket out of the refrigerator and offered it to David.

One tiny piece of chicken won't hurt.

Yes, it will. It's loaded with fat and grease.

She chewed her lower lip, watching David put a crispy brown thigh onto a plate. He added a breast, a drumstick and two biscuits, then heaped mashed potatoes next to them and doused the entire plate with smooth, creamy gravy.

It looks so good . . . just one little piece.

Fine. And you can look like a fat white blob on your wedding day.

C.J. swallowed hard and battled the overwhelming temptation to reach out and break off a piece of the succulent, crumbly breading.

Just one little taste.

Well, maybe just a taste. Just to get this craving out of your system.

But before she could reach out, Lila moved in, covered the plate with a paper towel and put it into the microwave. "Go ahead and sit down, David. You must be tired after that drive," she said, slamming the oven door and setting the timer. "I'll take this out when it's ready. Why don't you have some Pepsi, or a beer? Oh, and for dessert, I bought those cupcakes you love so much—the cherry ones with the crunchy sprinkles. And, Clara Joy, I bought your favorite fat-free ranch dressing, too.''

"Thanks," C.J. mumbled.

She walked over to the fridge and reached into the crisper for the lettuce.

"Clara Joy Clarke, I haven't seen you in months!"

What's that supposed to mean? she wondered defensively. *That I haven't been to Mass at St. Michael's since last Christmas? Well, I don't even live around here anymore.*

But she hadn't been to Mass in Chicago, much, either.

And she always had the feeling that Father Manelli could read her mind.

Welcome to a good old-fashioned Catholic guilt session, she thought wryly.

"It's good to see you again, Father," she said, and cleared her throat.

He clasped her hand. Somehow, though it was a hundred degrees outside, his fingers were cold and dry. She was so nervous that hers would have been clammy if this were January. The humidity made them so sweaty that she had to keep wiping them on the skirt her mother had "suggested" she wear.

"Oh, um, Father, this is my fiancé, David Griffin."

David, looking neat and combed, if a little flushed, stepped forward and shook the priest's hand. "Nice to meet you, Father."

"And you. You've got yourself a wonderful gal, there, David."

"I know."

"Well, why don't you come into my office and have a seat." Father Manelli stepped back and motioned them to proceed down the hall.

C.J. hadn't been back in the rectory in years—not since her high school days, when she'd been active in the parish youth organization. The place hadn't changed a bit. Same dark paneling, same brown indoor-outdoor-style carpet, same religious pictures and statues on every wall and surface.

Father Manelli escorted them into his small office and closed the door behind them. "Take a seat," he said, waving a hand at the two chairs facing his desk. He sat in the brown fake leather chair on the other side and leaned forward, propping his chin on his clasped hands.

"So," he said, studying them.

C.J. wiped her palms on her skirt and folded her hands in her lap. She glanced at David. He looked calm. How could he always look so calm? On the way over here in the car, she'd been practically panicking, and David had seemed placid as usual.

She looked back at Father Manelli. He was still watching them, and she couldn't read the expression on his face. She gave him a little smile, felt foolish and looked down at her lap.

"So," the priest said at last, "you want to get married."

"Yes," David agreed, "that's what we want to do."

C.J. just nodded.

"And, you," the priest said to David, "aren't Catholic. Correct?"

The way he said it, you'd think he'd concluded that David was some sort of criminal.

C.J. said, "He's *half*-Catholic," as though she were trying to protect him, and then wished she hadn't when she saw the expression on David's face.

"I'm not half-Catholic," he corrected, still sounding composed. "My father is Catholic. My mother was Jewish. I'm Jewish."

"But not practicing?" Father Manelli asked.

"You could say that. I don't go to temple very much these days, but I do consider myself a Jew."

"I see."

C.J. wondered if Father Manelli would have approved of David more if he *were* practicing. This way, it sounded as if David didn't care one way or another about religion.

"Well, Clara Joy, David...the church is happy that you two have found love and commitment. We uphold those values and applaud young people who embark on that difficult, bittersweet journey called marriage. It is, as you know, Clara Joy, one of the seven blessed sacraments."

She nodded, feeling as though he were going to ask her to name the rest of them, like he used to back in religious instruction classes. Irrationally, her mind started counting them off. *Baptism...First Communion...*

"And we are glad that you have come here, to your home parish, Clara Joy, to make arrangements for this marriage."

C.J. glanced up at that, and then at David.

"We'd like to have an interfaith ceremony, Father," she blurted, "on neutral turf."

The priest's expression didn't change.

"I see" was all he said.

When he didn't speak again, just sat there watching them, C.J. started talking to fill the silence. "We thought we could have a priest and a rabbi...I mean, *you,* if you'll do it, and a rabbi, and we could have it someplace nice...someplace here in town—we're going to look at places later...." She trailed off helplessly.

David jumped in to her rescue. "We both feel, Father Manelli, that having both our religions represented in a nondenominational setting would be the best option."

"But, David, you understand that you *can* be married in the church," Father Manelli said.

"I know that I *can,* but I don't believe a rabbi will agree to perform a ceremony within the Catholic church. And I wouldn't feel comfortable being married in one," he added firmly.

"Father, we don't *have* to get married in the church, in order to have our marriage recognized, do we?" C.J. asked. "I mean, it's not a..." She wanted to say *law,* but changed it to, "A requirement?"

"Normally it is a requirement, but there is an exception that fits your case. When one of the parties isn't Christian, a priest can perform the ceremony elsewhere."

"That's great!" C.J. interjected before Father Manelli continued. "I, however, cannot agree to perform your ceremony. I'm sorry, Clara Joy."

There was an awkward silence.

Then David said, "We understand."

Father Manelli nodded, then went on, "You're aware that there is a condition to which you both must agree? You'll have to sign a statement acknowledging that you'll raise your children as Catholics."

C.J.'s eyebrows shot up. "We have to *sign* something?"

"That's right."

Rage bubbled up inside of her, and she bit her lip to hold it back.

David cleared his throat. "That's fine," he said calmly.

Father Manelli stood. "Good. I'll be right back. I've got to go get Clara Joy's records and we can start filling out the paperwork."

As soon as he'd walked out, C.J. turned to David. "Why did you tell him we'll sign? We haven't even discussed *having* children, let alone how they'll be raised."

"Keep your voice down. I know we haven't. But I don't mind signing something like that. I'm not that religious, and besides, children usually are raised in their mother's faith."

"But *I'm* not that religious, either," C.J. hissed. "I hardly ever go to church."

David shrugged. "So what's the big deal, then?"

"Why don't we get married by a justice of the peace and forget all of this?"

"Because having a rabbi there is important to me. Why don't we have a Jewish ceremony if you don't care about the Catholic part?"

She considered that.

"Well?" He looked at her.

"I guess I am a little bit religious," she said quietly. "I wouldn't feel right having a strictly Jewish ceremony. But, David—"

"We'll work it out." He reached over and picked up her left hand. Her diamond ring twinkled up at them.

Diamonds are forever, C.J. thought, and squeezed his warm fingers. "You're right. We'll work it out."

Saturday night, C.J. lay in bed in her old room, wide-awake even though she was utterly exhausted.

The meeting with Father Manelli had been a breeze compared to what had happened later. C.J., David and her parents had driven all over creation, examining country clubs and restaurants and banquet halls that Lila had scouted earlier in the week. Each time they all climbed back into the car after taking the tour and listening to the manager's pitch, C.J. had vetoed the place with a flat "I hate it."

Lila would invariably say, "But *why,* Clara Joy? A wedding there would be lovely!"

And then C.J. would have to shrug and tell her, "I don't know *why.* I just hate it."

She'd started to feel like a spoiled brat as the ordeal continued into the evening hours, but she kept reminding herself that this was her *wedding,* a once-in-a-lifetime event, and she had a right to have at least *some* say about it.

By the time they met Kyle back at home for dinner, C.J. was on the verge of tears—worn-down by stress, exhaustion, hunger and the suffocating heat.

David, who had found something optimistic to say about every one of the places, had squeezed her hand and whispered, "Don't worry. We'll find someplace."

All through a cold supper of pasta and tossed salads and watermelon, C.J. had brooded. And afterward, when her father had suggested that they play Scrabble, she'd tried to back out, but no one would let her. At least she'd won two out of the three games.

And at least no one had tried to spell out the word *bride*. Or *wedding*. Or *fiasco*.

But now, as C.J. lay awake and restless, she couldn't stop thinking about it.

She didn't want her marriage ceremony to be performed in some restaurant, with people sitting in folding chairs and cooking smells wafting in. Or in the banquet room at her father's Moose Lodge, with the giant, mounted head of an animal overlooking the proceedings. Her father's joke that they could decorate the antlers with crepe paper and tissue flowers hadn't helped.

She'd hoped for a more ethereal setting.

Such as the beach, with waves crashing and sea gulls chattering.

Or even someplace stylish and urbane, such as one of the renovated loft spaces in the Loop. She'd been to a wedding in one of them, and the brick walls and wooden floors had lent a stark class to the scene. The bride's mother, who was an interior decorator, had draped clouds of white tulle everywhere, and the small round tables were set with lacy white cloths, white candles and white roses in porcelain vases. And dozens of white helium balloons had been set adrift.

It was like being in heaven.

It wouldn't even be so bad if just C.J.'s *reception* were going to be in a restaurant or the Moose Lodge. But she and David would actually have to be *married* there. She'd have to walk down an aisle there.

The thought of it was just so. . . *horrendous*.

She flopped onto her stomach and bunched her pillow under her chin.

If only they had been able to make their wedding plans back in June, as they'd intended. In the summer or fall, they could have an outdoor wedding just about anywhere. Hell, a parking lot was more romantic than the Moose Lodge.

But now it was too late. There weren't many options for a winter wedding.

And David really wanted to be married before the end of the year. Actually, so did she. This limbo time was already making her crazy. She was anxious to start a new life with him.

And get this damn wedding over with.

Oh, God. Listen to yourself.

How could she be thinking this way about an event she'd always thought would be so meaningful and beautiful that she'd want to relive it forever?

Because so far, planning it had been nothing but one giant headache.

And they hadn't even set the date yet.

C.J. flopped over onto her back again and sighed.

She didn't know what had possessed her to get up and go to church with her parents. Now that they were scurrying up the steps, with the bells ringing in the tower overhead, she regretted it. Father Manelli was notoriously long-winded, and there was no air-conditioning at St. Michaels.

Sure enough, as soon as C.J. stepped inside, she felt the warm air closing in, along with a stifling cloud of incense, dust and an overwhelming blend of strong perfumes and colognes.

Her father led the way to their usual pew near the front, and stepped back to let C.J., her mother and Kyle file in. They all knelt, the familiar blond-wigged organist started playing and C.J. said a brief prayer, asking God to forgive her for not going to church lately.

Then she rose with the congregation as Father Manelli and a cluster of robed Eucharistic ministers and altar boys formed a procession down the aisle.

She actually felt a little better as the Mass went on. More peaceful, as though the familiar rituals were soothing her. Sunlight streamed through the stained-glass windows, highlighting the polished old wood of the pews and seeming to spotlight the altar.

Maybe I should come to church more often, C.J. thought, looking around. She spotted her old high school friend, Sara Rausch, across the way with her parents and brothers. And there was C.J.'s old dentist, and the boy she'd once had a crush on in grade school.

She wondered if David might come to church with her sometimes, if she decided she wanted to go. She hadn't bothered to wake him this morning, but maybe once in a while they could do this.

She settled back in the pew and tried to listen as Father Manelli droned on in his homily, but found her mind wandering.

It was the word *homosexuals* that snapped her back to full attention. What was that? Something about people who insisted on going against the teachings of Jesus and the Bible. How their sinful behavior must not be accepted. How "we must bind together, as Catholics and as brothers and sisters, to show them that the life-style they have chosen is wrong."

C.J. tightened her hands into fists so that her nails dug into her palms.

Father Manelli continued to advise the congregation that they must guide their errant brothers and sisters back to the righteous path.

C.J. did her best to tune him out, but by the end of his sermon, she was seething.

After Mass, in the car, she burst out, "I can't believe that in this day and age, people just sit there and listen while someone lectures against homosexuality!"

Her parents and Kyle turned to look at her, surprised.

"What do you expect?" Kyle asked blandly. "This is church, not some liberal rally."

"I'm disgusted," C.J. said, flopping back against the seat, folding her arms and shaking her head. "I thought the Bible said to love one another—not to condemn someone who has a different life-style. This is why I don't go to church anymore.''

She ignored the little voice inside that reminded her that the biggest reason she hadn't been going to church was that she was lazy. Until now, she hadn't even considered the politics of her religion.

"Clara Joy, don't get so excited," her mother said. "You may not agree with everything the Catholic church teaches—I don't, either—but that doesn't mean you shouldn't go."

"Yes, it does. I'm not going to be a hypocrite."

Lila shook her head. "Clara Joy, just because David isn't a Christian doesn't mean you can't embrace your own religion even after you're married."

"*What?* What are you talking about? What does *David* have to do with this? I'm talking about the Catholic religion's intolerant view of homosexuality." She looked to Kyle for help, but he only shrugged.

"Why bother getting so worked up? It's no big deal," he said blandly.

"Yes, it is a big deal. In fact, I'm really thinking twice about having a religious wedding ceremony at all."

She saw her father's hands clench the steering wheel more tightly, but he said nothing. He rarely got involved in family disputes.

Her mother, on the other hand, whirled around and looked horrified. "Oh, Clara Joy, you don't mean that," Lila said.

"I don't? What's a priest going to think of Seamus? He's going to be my 'man of honor,' you know, and he's going to be there with a male date. What if, during the ceremony, the priest starts in on the evils of homosexuality?"

Kyle snickered and her mother shook her head. "That won't happen. Please, Clara Joy, calm down. Your wedding is going to be lovely. You'll see."

C.J. just stared out the window and wondered how life had grown so complicated.

* * *

"Hello, Mom?" C.J. said into the phone.

"Clara Joy! I've been waiting for you to call. How was your trip back to Chicago? Was there much traffic?"

"It wasn't that bad."

David raised an eyebrow at her.

She shrugged and shook her head. Why bother telling Lila that it had been pouring rain the entire trip and the Dan Ryan Expressway was bumper-to-bumper because of an accident? C.J. wanted to get this phone call over with as quickly as possible, with no distractions.

"Well?" Lila prodded. "Did you make up your minds about where you want to have the wedding?"

"Yes. We discussed it in the car and we've decided on the Claypool House," C.J. said decisively.

It was the best of the lot—a nice restaurant in an old stone house on Main Street. As David had optimistically pointed out, it had a nice carved wooden staircase that C.J. could descend on her father's arm, and they could be married in front of the enormous fireplace in the dining room.

"The Claypool House? That sounds wonderful. I'll call them now."

"But, Mom, it's Labor Day," she protested. She glanced at David, who was removing dirty clothes from his suitcase and tossing them into a laundry basket. "The restaurant is probably really busy tonight."

"Henry won't mind." He was the balding, bespectacled manager who had given them the spiel about what the Claypool House could offer them.

"Fine," C.J. said. Might as well stop dragging her heels.

"Now, let's see—he said he had the last two Saturdays in December open, didn't he? Which one do you want?"

"The one between Christmas and New Year's."

"Good. I'll call you right back."

"We're at David's. Do you have the number?"

"Yes, it's right here. Wait by the phone."

"Right." C.J. sighed and hung up the phone. "My mother's calling now to reserve the date."

"Good." David held up one of her shirts. "Does this get washed or dry-cleaned?"

"Washed. I guess it'll be nice. Getting married at the Claypool House, I mean. Don't you think?"

"Of course it'll be nice, C.J. Marrying you would be more than 'nice' *anywhere.*"

She smiled. "You're so sweet. I'll be right back."

She went into the tiny bathroom and washed up. She was brushing her long, curly brown hair back into a ponytail when she heard the phone ring.

"David?" she called around the barrette she was clenching in her teeth.

"I've got it."

She heard him pick it up. It was her mother.

"No, she's in the other room," David was saying. "Yes, you're right—I do have only one room. But she's actually in the bathroom."

C.J. rolled her eyes and fastened the barrette around her hair. Then she put the brush down and headed into the other room to rescue David. She motioned for him to hand over the phone, but he held up an index finger and mouthed, "Wait."

After listening for a moment, he said, "Well then, how about a Friday night? For what? Oh, that's right. It's Christmas party season."

C.J. frowned. "What's the matter?" she asked David.

He covered the mouthpiece and said quietly, "Both of those Saturdays have been booked."

"*When?* We were just there two days ago and they were open!"

David shrugged and motioned for her to be quiet. "Well, then, if we have to consider November, or even January, I guess we can. No. I know, but—they are?"

"They are *what?*" C.J. asked.

"Closed for the whole month of January. And before and after that, they're booked," David told her. "Right through spring."

C.J. plunked herself down on the couch and shook her head. "Tell her to try our second choice, then," she said. "It was Gordon's."

"She wants you to try Gordon's," David told Lila. "No. Yes, we know they only had that one date open. Hopefully, no one grabbed it since we were there. Right. We'll wait right here."

He hung up and looked at C.J. "She's going to call Gordon's."

"I hate Gordon's."

"Oh, come on, C.J. You admitted in the car that it has a nice view from that plate-glass window in the dining room. We can have the ceremony right in front of it."

"I guess."

"Don't mope. It'll be fine." He reached into the suitcase again and held up a pair of her shorts. "Do these go with the light clothes or the dark?"

"Light. What else did my mother say?"

"Nothing much. She said that Henry was sorry about filling those dates, but he had no choice. First come, first served."

The phone rang again and both of them jumped. C.J. grabbed it.

"Hello?"

"Clara Joy?"

"Did you get Gordon's?"

"No. That date is booked now."

"What the heck is going on? Did a sea of engaged couples descend upon the town over the weekend?"

"Apparently," her mother said grimly. "I'm going to call Ella Tibbio over at Giardello's and see what they have open."

"No!" C.J. protested. "I hate that place."

"Clara Joy, the food is wonderful and they have lots of room to set up rows of chairs for the ceremony."

"I know, but I hate the decor. It's so tacky. I can't get married there."

"Well, then, what do you want to do?"

C.J. looked at David expectantly.

"The Orchard Grill was our third choice, right?" she asked him.

"Right."

"Call the Orchard Grill," she told her mother. "I'll wait by the phone."

She hung up and looked at David. "I *hate* the Orchard Grill," she muttered.

"C.J...."

"Well, I do. It's so *dark* in there."

"It'll be fine."

"*If* they even have any dates available. Weren't they pretty booked?"

"I think they were."

"Great."

A few minutes later, another call from Lila confirmed it. The Orchard Grill was booked until summer.

There was nothing to do but try choice number four.

Which also turned out to be booked.

So they worked their way down the list until they reached the bottom.

And found the only place that had an opening in the near-enough future.

The last Saturday in December.

The Moose Lodge.

Four

On a rare weeknight in the middle of September, C.J. and Seamus found themselves home alone together.

No David—he was at a business dinner. And no Chad—he was working late on an important case.

"Hey," Seamus said, coming back into the kitchen after changing out of his work clothes. "Why don't we order a pizza with the works, buy some beer and rent some old Tom Cruise movie like *The Outsiders?*"

"Why Tom Cruise?" C.J. asked, looking up from the notebook she was writing in at the kitchen table.

"Because I love Tom. He's a beautiful man."

"So is Chad."

"True. But that doesn't stop me from looking at others with lust." Seamus lit a cigarette.

"I thought you and Chad decided that you were committed to each other."

"We did. That doesn't mean I can't *look.* I mean, you do it, right?"

"Do what?"

"Look at other men."

"I do not."

"Oh, don't give me that." Seamus sat down across from her and plunked his ashtray on the table. "You mean to tell me that you work at a meat market like Razzles every single night and don't even check out the guys?"

C.J. shrugged. "No." She was engaged. She wasn't supposed to be checking out guys.

"You do, too," Seamus told her, exhaling a stream of smoke. "Don't give me that innocent look."

"Seamus," she protested, shaking her head. "I'm getting married."

"So?"

"So, my lusting days are over."

She closed the notebook, where she'd been making a list of people she wanted to invite to the wedding. So far, she was in the hundreds, and that didn't include any of David's relatives or her own.

"Hey, do you ever think about Dig Lawrence?" Seamus asked abruptly, raising an eyebrow at her.

"No! Of course I don't. At least, not in *that* way."

"Sore subject?"

"Very. Yet somehow you happen to bring it up every single time you and I are alone together."

"Sorry." Seamus took another drag. "Did you ever tell David about it?"

"What, are you crazy? Of course I didn't tell David."

"Why not? It happened before you were engaged."

"I know, but . . . I can't tell him. Not for a long time."

"So what are you thinking? That someday, when the two of you are old and gray, you're going to say, 'Oh, by the way, honey, I once had a one-night stand with Dig Lawrence'?"

"Something like that."

Seamus shook his head. "Don't tell him."

"Why not?"

"Because it's not going to do any good."

"I owe it to David to be honest."

"You just want to clear your conscience."

C.J. stood and picked up her notebook. "Why are we even talking about this? It's no big deal. I'm hungry."

"Me, too. Pizza?"

"You're supposed to be eating healthy," she said gently.

"So what? I always eat healthy. I'm *gagging* on healthy food these days. I had a grapefruit for breakfast and a salad for lunch. No sugar on the grapefruit, low-fat dressing on the salad. How much more healthy can you get?''

''Seamus...''

''C.J., if I'm going to get sick, I'm going to get sick.''

''That's not true. You know damn well that your doctor told you that eating healthy makes a big difference.''

''Well, why prolong life if you're not going to enjoy it?'' he asked pointedly, looking her in the eye. ''I'd rather have six happy, fulfilling months left than a dismal year or two of sacrificing everything that matters to me.''

''Okay.''

''You want to tell me what good life is if you can't eat a damned potato chip every now and then?''

C.J. was taken aback by his vehement tone. She didn't know what to say. He'd been so good up until now, rarely complaining as he gave up the junk food he'd loved and made a point to work out daily, take vitamins and get to bed at a decent hour. The one thing he had steadfastly refused to attempt was giving up cigarettes.

Now he inhaled the one in his hand as though it were a lifeline.

He looked her in the eye. ''Well?''

''Pizza,'' she agreed, ''with the works.''

''That's all right. Thank you for your time,'' David said, and plunked the phone back into its cradle.

''What'd he say?'' C.J. asked, looking up from the bridal magazine she'd been pretending to read.

''He said that even though he's a Reform rabbi, he doesn't condone interfaith weddings. He asked me if I had thought this through carefully and he offered to meet with me for some 'counseling.''' David shook his head and crossed the rabbi's name off the list that was scribbled on a piece of yellow legal paper. ''Twelve down, one more left to try. Rabbi Sam Krantz.''

David grimly punched out the numbers on the telephone and held up crossed fingers. "Maybe this one will work out."

"Maybe." But she doubted it. She'd spent four hours this morning calling what seemed like every priest in Illinois, and had come up with nothing.

"It's ringing," David announced, as though that were a good sign.

C.J. nodded and went back to her magazine. She flipped a page and studied a simple white dress in a fashion layout. Hmm. This one wouldn't be so bad if it weren't for that puffy thing around the neck. . . .

"Hello, yes, I'd like to speak with Rabbi Krantz, please." David was saying into the phone.

C.J. glanced up at him.

His smile faded. "He is? Uh, well, do you know when he'll be back in town? . . . That long, huh? . . . All right . . . Yes . . . No, that's okay. I'll just call him back then. Thank you." He hung up and looked at C.J.

"Well?"

"He's in California till the first of October."

"Great."

David tossed his pen and paper onto the table and leaned back in his chair. "This is becoming difficult."

"'Difficult'? Tell me about it. Calling fifty priests was no picnic, either."

"Don't worry. We'll find someone."

"We need *two* someones—a priest and a rabbi."

"We'll find them."

"David, why don't we just give up and get married by a justice of the peace?"

He looked at her. "C.J., you know how I feel about that."

"I know. But I wonder why we're knocking ourselves out to have a religious ceremony when we're not even all that religious." She put her magazine down on the couch and walked over to stand by him. "Do we really need to go through all this trouble? I mean, half the priests I've spoken to and half the rabbis you've reached have tried to talk us out of getting married in the first place.''

''I know, but what do you expect? They're not going to encourage us to marry out of faith.'' David pulled her down onto his lap and patted her arm. ''Don't worry, C.J. No matter what, we're going to get married and it's going to be great.''

''The wedding?''

''The marriage. The wedding . . . well, it *might* be great.''

She groaned, and he grinned and kissed her on the cheek. ''I love you. That's all that counts, right?'' he asked.

''I love you, too. But it's not *all* that counts. We're never going to find an agreeable priest and an agreeable rabbi.''

''Sure we will.''

''I think we should just drop the whole idea and have a civil ceremony.''

''I don't *want* a civil ceremony,'' he said forcefully.

She stared at him. ''I didn't think you were all that religious.''

''Well, maybe I don't go to temple, but, C.J., it's important to me to have a rabbi at our wedding.''

''Why?''

He shrugged. ''It just is.''

She hesitated. They had been through this before. And once again, the closed expression on David's face told her not to pursue it.

''Don't worry,'' he said after a moment. ''We'll find a priest and we'll find a rabbi and we'll get married.''

''You make it sound so simple.''

''You make it sound impossible.''

C.J. sighed. ''That's what it feels like.''

''Don't worry. I promise it's going to work out.''

''How can you promise?''

''I just can.'' He kissed her again. ''Okay?''

She shrugged. ''Okay.''

* * *

"Of course I'll be in your wedding," Becky said happily, leaning across the small table to hug C.J.

"Me, too," Jessica put in, smiling and tossing her silky blond hair over her shoulder. "Although this is starting to feel like the old 'always a bridesmaid' thing."

Becky and C.J. looked at each other.

"What's wrong, Jess?" C.J. asked, spreading her linen napkin on her lap and picking up her water goblet.

"Oh, it's no big deal. It's just that Jake sort of told me, the other night, that he has no intention of getting married. Ever."

Jake was her live-in boyfriend, and it hadn't been so long ago that C.J. was insanely jealous over his and Jessica's cozy relationship. That was back when David had been dragging his heels about making a commitment.

"Don't worry, Jess. I didn't think David would ever come around, and look at us now."

Jessica shrugged. "I always knew David would marry you, C.J. He's been crazy about you from day one. But Jake is different."

"Oh, come on, Jess," C.J. said. "The guy is in love with you."

"Maybe. But that doesn't make him the marrying type."

"Maybe he just has cold feet, Jessica," Becky said in her quiet, sensible way.

"Nah. He said he loves me, but he can't see himself taking the plunge." Jessica reached for her glass of mineral water and lifted it. "How about a toast, though? After all, this is supposed to be a celebratory lunch. Here's to C.J. and David—at least *someone's* going to live happily ever after."

Becky and C.J. raised their wineglasses. They clinked them together, then sipped.

Becky set her glass down and turned to C.J. "So, how are the wedding plans coming?"

"Let's just say, not even as well as could be expected," C.J. said.

"What's the matter?" Jessica asked. "Trouble in paradise?"

"No, David and I are fine. But we can't seem to find a willing rabbi *or* a willing priest. And David's stepmother sent him a guest list yesterday that was a yard long. She wants to invite everybody and their gardener. And my mother is threatening to wear turquoise taffeta with sequins. And—"

"Don't worry," Becky cut in. "Things will work out."

"Yeah, right. At least David called his dad last night and told him the list would have to be cut, and he said he'd take care of it. I talked to him, too. I've never met him in person, but he sounded really sweet and calm and reassuring."

Becky smiled. "Like father, like son, huh?"

"C.J., you two have been engaged for over a year now. Aren't you going to visit David's hometown and meet his family before the wedding?" Jessica asked.

"Actually, I am. On Columbus Day weekend." C.J. shrugged. "I have two weeks to lose thirty pounds so they won't think David's engaged to a cow."

"C.J., you look great. You're not a cow," Becky said loyally.

"Yeah, right."

"Did you find a wedding dress yet?" Jessica reached for the bread basket the waiter had just set in the middle of the table.

"Nope. That's problem number one hundred and one, though. It can wait." C.J. swallowed hard as she watched her skinny friend slather a giant chunk of warm bread with two pats of butter.

"Are you kidding? You'd better get moving. You can't just pick out any old white dress off the rack, you know," Jessica said, then took a big bite of her bread. "Mmm. This is so good. I'm starving. And how about us? Have you given any thought to the bridesmaids' dresses yet?''

"Not yet." C.J. downed half her glass of water, trying to fill her empty stomach. She'd ordered a garden salad, no dressing, and if the waiter didn't bring it soon, she was going to start devouring that bread.

"Why don't we go shopping some day this week?" Jessica asked, polishing off her first piece of bread and reaching for the basket again. "Lord knows I'm free. Jake has been spending a lot of time at work. He's involved in some new case that's taking up all his time."

C.J. shrugged. The thought of shopping with Jessica was about as appealing as shopping with her mother would be. Jess tended to have extravagant taste. And besides, what might look stunning on her sleek model's figure wouldn't necessarily flatter the other bridesmaids—especially pudgy Tina St. John.

"So, C.J., have you and David figured out where you're going to live yet?" Becky asked.

"Right now, that's the least of our worries. I guess we'll go apartment hunting in a month or so." She fiddled with her spoon, vaguely noticing a film of leftover crud on it.

"What's the matter? You seem kind of down." Jessica peered at her over the bud vase on the table. "If I were planning a wedding, I'd be on top of the world."

"Yeah, well, I thought I would be, too. But it's kind of..."

"Stressful?" Becky supplied.

"Exactly. Somehow, I'd always thought things would be perfect if I were getting married. But now it seems like every time I turn around, there's a new problem to deal with."

"Don't worry," Becky said. "Things will work out, no matter what. The important thing is that you're getting married."

"You sound like David."

"Then listen to him." Becky patted her hand. "Your wedding will be beautiful."

C.J. pictured the Moose Lodge, and dueling men of the cloth, and Lila in a mother-of-the-bride gown.

"Yeah" was all she said.

A torrential rainstorm had kept the usual Monday night Razzles crowd home, and C.J. was bored out of her mind.

She'd watched back-to-back sitcoms on the television over the bar before switching it to the Monday night football game. She'd lined the glasses up in perfect rows on the shelves, and polished the long wooden bar so many times that it was gleaming like one of those tables in a furniture polish commercial.

Now there was nothing left to do but hang out with Steve, the other bartender, and she hated doing that. He was a right-wing bigot who loved to stir up controversy. Though C.J. always vowed not to let him get to her, he invariably made some inflammatory remark that worked its way under her skin and started a debate rolling.

Right now, as she brushed by him to get herself a glass of water from the tap, he clucked his tongue and turned a page in the newspaper he was reading.

She knew he wanted her to ask him what he was reading.

She ignored him and started walking toward the other end of the bar.

"Look at this," he said, shaking his head and grabbing her arm to stop her.

She didn't look.

He waved the newspaper in her face. "Can you believe it?"

She sighed. "What?"

"This faggot is screaming discrimination because his landlord kicked him out."

She clenched her jaw and turned her back.

"Oh, come on now, C.J., you're not going to take his side, are you? The guy is a pansy. Look at the way he's got his sweater tied around his hips. No wonder the landlord gave him the boot."

C.J. sighed and walked away. She leaned her elbows on the bar and put her chin in her hands, surveying the crowd. There were a few couples scattered at tables, and some of the regulars dotted the stools lining the bar.

One of them, a beer-bellied welder named Stan, caught her eye and winked. C.J. smiled briefly. The guy was a depressing cliché, with a just-cashed paycheck in his pocket, a wandering eye and a wife and five kids at home.

The door opened and someone blew in on a gust of wind and rain. C.J. didn't recognize him until he was right in front of the bar.

Dig Lawrence.

She hadn't seen him in over a year.

His eyes widened. "C.J.? What are you doing here?"

"Working," she said, noting that he was as gorgeous as ever, even though he looked a little tired and his glossy dark hair was wet and windblown.

"Moonlighting, huh?"

"Not quite."

"What happened to your job at the television station?"

"I quit a long time ago," she told him briefly, and slapped a cocktail napkin down in front of him. "What do you want? We have two-for-one Molsons on special."

He nodded. "A Molson sounds good."

"No dry martini?" she asked, remembering that that was his usual. It was what he'd been drinking the last time they'd bumped into each other here.

He just laughed and said, "Not tonight."

She shoved the disconcerting memory of that night out of her mind and turned around to get his beer.

When she brought it over to where he'd settled on a bar stool, he handed her a twenty. "So you're working here at Razzles, huh?"

"Looks that way." She took two steps to the register, rang it in and went to hand him his change. He motioned for her to set it on the bar.

"How do you like it?" he asked, catching her before she could slip away.

"Bartending?" She paused. "It's all right."

He nodded sympathetically. "I've done my share of drudge work, too. But those days are long behind me—I hope."

C.J. couldn't help noticing how extraordinarily good-looking he was. His face was perfect, with a chiseled jaw and cheekbones and full lips... Those lips. Mmm. She still remembered how amazing those lips had felt on hers.

Dig took off his rain-splotched trenchcoat and C.J. noticed how the muscles in his arms and chest bulged against the expensive fabric of his plain ivory shirt.

Most of her night with Dig was a drunken blur in her memory, but she did recall running her fingers over those strong arms and that sculpted chest.

Stop that. Think of David.

But the image of her fiancé wouldn't come. Suddenly, all she could think of was Dig, panting and moving above her in her shadowy bedroom. She felt herself growing flushed and again started to walk away.

"Hey, where are you going?"

"I have to...uh..." She looked around. The few other people sitting at the bar were taken care of, and Steve was leaning against the opposite end, reading his paper.

"Why don't you keep me company?" Dig asked. "I hate sitting in a bar alone."

"Then how come you're here by yourself?"

"I'm waiting for someone, actually."

"Oh." C.J. picked up a rag and started wiping down the polished surface a few feet away from him.

"You know, you look like you've lost weight," Dig commented.

She hadn't—and she didn't know whether to be insulted by his comment, or flattered.

Dig reached out and closed his hand over hers. "Hey, what's this?" He raised her hand and peered at it. "An engagement ring?"

C.J. nodded. The contact with his warm grasp made something deep inside of her perform a little somersault.

"You're getting married?"

"That's usually what an engagement ring means," she tried to say lightly, pulling her hand from his clutches.

"Who's the lucky guy?"

"David."

"David?"

"My boyfriend. You've met him."

"Oh. Right. At your apartment that time."

C.J. had thrown a get-together for the people involved in a reality-television feature she was taping for work. Dig had been one of the participants. In fact, C.J. was fully aware that probably the only reason he had ever given her the time of day was because he'd hoped she could make him a star.

"So C. J. Clarke is getting married," Dig said, shaking his head and sipping his beer. "Congratulations."

"Thanks."

She didn't like the way he was looking at her over the rim of his glass. Like he was remembering.

"So did you ever tell him?" he asked after a moment, setting his drink down carefully.

"Tell who what?" she asked promptly, even though she knew exactly what he meant.

"Tell your fiancé what happened that night while he was out of town on business," he asked with a little grin.

C.J. knew he was flirting, that he flirted with everyone. She was well-acquainted with that charming quality of his. But there was something intimate and sexy and riveting about his tone and his expression, and she felt helplessly turned on.

Sensations she had deliberately buried for months suddenly bombarded her.

She tasted Dig's probing tongue, heard him moaning and panting into her ear. And she felt his lean, hard body pressing and shuddering against hers.

Until now, she'd forced herself to recall only the shame and guilt of that long-ago night she'd spent with him. Until now, she hadn't let herself remember pleasure.

And there had been pleasure.

She stared at him, wondering if he knew what she was thinking—if he was thinking the same thing.

"Well, did you?" he asked, still watching her.

She blinked. "Did I what?"

"Tell David."

She cleared her throat and looked away. "Oh. No."

"Why not?"

Before she could answer him, someone slid onto the stool next to Dig's and said, "Hi. Sorry I'm late."

C.J. tried not to watch as Dig greeted the woman with a lingering kiss.

Then he turned to her and said, "C.J., this is Holly. Holly, C. J. Clarke. C.J. produced that television news feature I was in last summer."

"Nice to meet you," C.J. said.

"You, too."

"Can I get you something to drink?"

"Chardonnay, please?"

C.J. nodded and walked away.

As she poured the wine, she realized that her hands were still trembling. Why did Dig Lawrence have to show up and stir up all of these unsettling feelings again?

How could she still be attracted to a man she didn't even *like* all that much?

She was getting married to David.

She *loved* David.

A person who was engaged and in love should fantasize only about their fiancé, shouldn't they?

So how come the only thing she could think about, all of a sudden, was the great sex she'd had with this person who was sitting at the bar with another woman?

Here she was, David's engagement ring weighing like a sinker on her finger, while the rest of her body tingled with the memory of what Dig Lawrence had done to it that night.

Get over it, she told herself grimly, plunking the wine bottle back on the shelf and picking up the glass. *It's time to move on. Just forget it ever happened.*

But she'd tried, and she still couldn't get over it.

Maybe there was only one way to put the fling with Dig behind her once and for all.

Tell David about it.

But of course, she couldn't do that.

At least, not until after they were married.

It was a gloomy, rainy Wednesday early in October, and C.J. was baking cookies for David.

At least, that was what she'd told herself when she'd gotten the idea. She had planned to go for a long run to work off the chicken wings she'd eaten at 2:00 a.m. after her shift at Razzles had ended. According to WZZ's lug-head meteorologist, it was supposed to be "a gorgeous Indian summer day—positively balmy."

When C.J. woke up and saw the dreary drizzle, she'd been at a loss. What was she going to do until five o'clock, when she had to go to work? And then she was struck by the memory of how, as a kid, on rainy October days, she would bake chewy, spicy, sugar-encrusted molasses cookies.

Of course, she wouldn't eat them herself. She was still on her prewedding diet, even though she hadn't lost much—all right, anything—yet.

No, she'd give the cookies to David. Maybe she'd even put them into a nice tin and tie them up with a ribbon. It had been awhile since she'd done something special for him.

As she headed for the kitchen, she tried to shrug off the thought that she was still feeling guilty about Dig.

She also tried to ignore the thought that she wanted to eat some molasses cookies herself.

She was just putting the first batch into the oven when the phone rang.

"Guess who's back in town?" David asked as soon as she'd picked up the receiver.

"Who?" she asked, pinching off a tiny piece of rich brown dough from what was left in the bowl. *Just a taste,* she told herself. *Just to make sure there's enough cinnamon.*

"Rabbi Sam Kranz, that's who."

"Really?" C.J. swallowed the raw cookie dough and focused on David. "Did you talk to him?"

"I called as soon as I got to the office, but he wasn't there. He just got back to me now."

"And?"

"And he said he'd be happy to perform our wedding ceremony!"

"That's great," C.J. said, trying to match David's enthusiasm. "Wow. I mean, that's really great."

"I know. Was I ever relieved. We're going to set up a meeting with him in a few weeks, after we get back from visiting my family. And here's the best part—he knows a number of priests who are willing to do interfaith ceremonies. He's going to check into it for us and let us know. C.J., our troubles are over."

"That's great," she said again.

"Listen, I have to run now. I've got a meeting upstairs in one minute. But I just wanted to call and tell you the news."

"Thanks, David," C.J. said.

"Talk to you later."

"Bye." She replaced the receiver in its cradle and stood staring out the kitchen window at the pouring rain.

David had found a rabbi. The rabbi was going to find a priest.

The ceremony was going to be exactly what he wanted it to be.

But what about what C.J. wanted?

What do you want? she asked herself, irritated.

She wasn't sure. She only knew that, now that the rabbi was on board, there was no chance of *not* having the interfaith ceremony.

Which was what they'd planned on having.

What *David* wanted.

But why?

She couldn't help feeling resentful that she had no idea what was motivating him. He was going to be her husband, and she didn't even know him well enough to understand what was going on in his mind.

She was going to marry the man, and she was afraid to even ask him about it, because if she did, she knew he'd get all quiet and closed off and she'd feel terrible, as though she'd tried to pry into something that was none of her business.

But it *was* her business, dammit!

She was going to be his wife.

And besides, this was her wedding, too. What if she decided she really didn't want a religious ceremony?

It's too late now, she told herself. *The wheels are in motion.*

With a sigh, she turned away from the window.

Her gaze immediately fell on the bowl of cookie dough on the table.

After only a moment's hesitation, she pulled up a chair and dug in.

Five

"What if your family hates me?"

"Relax. They won't hate you."

"What if they do?" C.J. stopped in the Jetway, causing the impatient businessman behind her to bump into her. "Oops, sorry," she said.

He just grunted and moved around her.

"Come on, C.J." David shifted her heavy carry-on bag to his other shoulder and grabbed her hand. "We're practically the last ones off the plane. They're going to think we missed the flight."

"Okay. Do I look all right?"

"You look beautiful."

Yeah, right.

"Okay," she said, "let's go."

She let David lead her down the Jetway and into the waiting area of Buffalo airport. The first person she saw was Fawn, who was hard to miss. She was wearing a big furry white hat and a sweeping red cape—and was clutching the arm of a man who was obviously David's father. Even if C.J. hadn't recognized him from David's photo album, she would have seen the resemblance between father and son. Bob Griffin had the same reddish hair—though his was streaked with gray—the same freckled face, the same earnest, calm demeanor.

Fawn immediately swept him over to C.J. and David. She captured them both in a cloud of perfume and powder and a strangling embrace. She clung to C.J.'s arm and turned to her husband. "Bob, meet your soon-to-be daughter-in-law!"

David's father nodded and clasped C.J.'s hand. "It's so nice to meet you at last," he said in a quiet voice.

"You, too," C.J. said, deciding instantly that she really liked this man.

He didn't have David's large brown eyes, but his pale blue ones radiated the same reassuring kindness. And while his smile didn't have the width or intensity of his son's trade-mark grin, C.J. sensed the same welcoming warmth that had wrapped around her when she first met David.

"Hey, where's Lauren?" David asked, setting the car-ryon down and rubbing his shoulder. "I thought she was coming to the airport with you."

"She wanted to, but she hasn't been feeling well and when Andy got home from work, he talked her into staying in to-night," Fawn said. "I had told her the same thing when I talked to her earlier today but she kept insisting that she wanted to be here to welcome you, Clara Joy."

"How sweet." C.J. knew that Andy was Lauren's hus-band and that Lauren was three months pregnant with their first child. Roxie, the older of the two sisters, was married to Lou, who was in the army, and they were stationed in Germany.

"Did you check luggage?" David's father asked.

"Yeah, one suitcase," David said, swinging the carryon over his shoulder again with a groan.

"David, that's so heavy. Let me help you," C.J. offered. The bag was crammed with the overflow of her clothing that wouldn't fit into her suitcase. She'd gone shopping last weekend and had bought what amounted to a whole new wardrobe to wear this weekend, even though she'd vowed earlier not to buy another thing until she'd lost weight. But she couldn't meet David's family in her tired old clothes.

"No, I've got it," David said easily. He grabbed her hand and gave her fingers a warm squeeze.

C.J. knew he was happy that she had met his father at last. He'd always promised her that Bob Griffin was nothing like the overbearing Fawn. In fact, David had never been able to figure out why his widowed father had married her. The only explanation was that he had been unbearably lonely. As David always pointed out, Fawn's incessant chatter had a way of filling up a room.

The four of them made their way down a long, window-lined corridor toward the baggage claim.

"So, how's the job going?" Bob asked David, and before C.J. knew it, the two men were walking ahead, deep in quiet conversation.

She was stuck with Fawn, who was prattling a mile a minute about the wedding.

"...And when I talked to your mother last night, she agreed that ivy would be just lovely on the head table, and she's going to talk to her garden club to see if they'll help with the decorations. And I saw a gown the other day in a bridal magazine that would be just perfect on you. It has a full skirt, which would be flattering on—oh, anyway, Clara Joy, I'll show you when we get home. Better bundle up," Fawn advised, turning back to her as they stepped onto a Down escalator. "It's in the twenties out there. In fact, they're predicting snow for tomorrow."

Great.

C.J.'s visions of an autumn-in-the-country weekend with David evaporated. What if one of those notorious Western New York October blizzards trapped her in the house with Fawn for days?

Better get used to her, she told herself. *The woman is going to be your mother-in-law for the rest of your life.*

At the bottom of the escalator, David had stopped and was waiting for her. He slipped his arm around C.J. as they walked toward the baggage claim, and she knew he was trying to shield her from Fawn.

"How are you making out?" he asked in her ear. "You okay?"

"I'm fine."

He's so sweet, C.J. thought, smiling at his profile. So sweet that everything—the wedding-planning craziness, and starving herself and dealing with nutty Fawn on a permanent basis—everything was worth it.

"And over there—" David nudged C.J. and pointed "—on the right, is the park where I lost my retainer that time I told you about."

"Oh, right." She peered at the broad clearing bordering Lake Erie. They were driving through Dunkirk now, David's hometown. It was a small city with grid-patterned streets that were lined with close-set wood-frame houses and huge old trees. There was a large harbor dotted with fishing boats and marinas, and at one end, an enormous, ugly power plant spewing gray smoke against the charcoal-gray night sky.

"Where's your house?" C.J. asked David as the car bumped over railroad tracks and the city street became a winding road.

"Out here, about a mile ahead."

C.J. stared out the window at the lakefront houses that were set back from the road. The farther out of town they went, the nicer and larger the homes became.

Within a few minutes, they were turning onto a long gravel driveway that passed between two large stone gateposts.

Fawn, in the front seat, interrupted her steady monologue directed toward David's father to turn around and say, "Well, this is it. Home, sweet home."

C.J. peered out the car window as they rounded the curved driveway and saw an expansive brick house with shuttered windows and a small, pillared stoop. It was centered on a large lot, with giant, sweeping trees and a gentle slope down to the water.

She knew David's family had been through some hard times when his mother was sick. David had worked his way through school, and there had been barely enough money to pay the medical bills. But obviously, Bob Griffin was now back on his feet financially—and then some. And down-to-earth David didn't seem to belong against this upscale backdrop, C.J. thought.

They all stepped out of the car and the freezing wind swept off the lake and snatched C.J.'s breath away.

"Go ahead with Fawn," David said, "and we'll get the luggage."

She didn't protest as his stepmother took her arm. "Come on, Clara Joy, I'll give you the grand tour."

Moments later, they were in a large foyer with a spotless white-and-black kitchen opening off in one direction, and a cozy-looking family room in the other.

"This is the back of the house," Fawn told her. "The front faces the lake."

"It's nice," C.J. said around chattering teeth.

"It is now." Fawn leaned forward and added in a conspiratorial tone, "Before I married Bob, the place was a mess. I don't mean to criticize a dead woman, and I'm sure his first wife was very sweet and a good mother, but she had no taste. I'll take your coat."

C.J. didn't say anything, just reluctantly handed it to Fawn and watched as she hung it in a closet by the door. "This is cedar lined," Fawn told her. "I had it custom designed."

"Nice."

The door blew open and David and his father came in.

"It definitely feels like snow," David said, shivering. He set down the suitcase he'd been carrying, took off his coat and tossed it over a wooden coat tree by the door. "Come on, C.J., and I'll show you around."

"Okay," she said, grateful to be spared Fawn's version of the grand tour.

Just before David led her into the kitchen, she saw his stepmother take his coat off the coat tree and hang it in the cedar-lined closet.

* * *

"You must be C.J.," said the petite, pretty, pregnant woman who walked in the front door Saturday morning just as C.J. was coming down the staircase. "I'm Lauren, and this is Andy," she added, gesturing at the tall blond man who was right behind her.

"Hi. It's nice to meet you." C.J. reached out to shake Lauren's hand, but was caught in an embrace instead.

"I have to hug you. Welcome to the family! We're so happy for you and David."

"Thanks," C.J. told her, touched by the genuine welcome.

"I wanted to come to the airport—" Lauren tossed her wavy reddish-brown hair "—but my husband wouldn't let me, big meanie."

"Laur, you know what the doctor said," he protested, shaking his head at her and lightly patting her barely protruding belly. He turned to C.J. "She's supposed to take it easy. She's been having a hard time with this pregnancy."

C.J. wondered if they knew David had told her that Lauren had been pregnant a few years ago, right after they'd gotten married, and that she'd had a miscarriage. They'd had a hard time conceiving again, according to David. No wonder Andy was looking at his wife as though she—and her cargo—were fragile and precious.

"So where is everyone?" Lauren asked, slipping out of her jacket and tossing it over the carved wooden coat tree.

"I don't know. David woke me up about a half hour ago and said he'd meet me downstairs."

"Well, I smell coffee, so they must—"

"Look, you're all right here! Clara Joy, Lauren, Andy, good morning," Fawn said, appearing in the foyer. "We're just about to sit down to breakfast."

"Good. I'm starved," Andy said.

"David and Bob are in the dining room. Go on in." Fawn moved over to the coat tree, removed Lauren's jacket and transferred it to her beloved cedar-lined closet.

David's sister looked irritated.

"How are you feeling, Lauren?" Fawn asked.

"Great," she said, and carefully wiped her feet on the mat by the door before venturing across the polished wooden floor toward the kitchen.

C.J. followed her past the sleek black appliances and the large breakfast nook. Lauren pointed at it. "We used to eat all our meals *there* before *she* came along," she muttered to C.J. under her breath.

C.J. wondered what kind of impact their father's remarriage had had on David and his sisters. David wasn't the type to discuss his feelings—and he certainly wouldn't trash his stepmother. He tended to focus on people's positive characteristics.

But C.J. had a feeling that his sister might give her an earful about Fawn if she got the opportunity.

They went into the formal dining room, with its heavy floor-length draperies framing the large windows that looked out over the lake. The long oval Queen Anne table was covered with white lace over rose-colored linen, and set with delicate rose-patterned china. The rose-colored candles in antique silver holders were lit.

David, his father, and Andy were clustered at one end of the table. David motioned C.J. to take the empty chair next to his.

"How'd you sleep?" he asked, patting her shoulder.

"Great." The canopy bed in their guest room was one of the most comfortable she'd ever slept in, and she'd drifted off effortlessly, snuggled beneath layers of smooth, sweet-smelling sheets and goose-down comforters.

"I hope everyone's hungry," Fawn said. "I had Emma make some of her famous spinach soufflé yesterday before she left."

"Emma?" C.J. looked at David. "Who's Emma?"

"The housekeeper," he said briefly, reaching for the coffee carafe and pouring some into his cup, then hers. "She's only here during the week. Want coffee?"

"Oh. Um, sure." C.J. lifted her cup and he filled it.

Fawn stood at the head of the table, serving soufflé, which she'd cut in dainty little wedges.

It was delicious, C.J. noted. But there wasn't really much to it.

Andy finished his in two bites, and so did Lauren. C.J. saw them exchange a glance. Then Lauren got up, went into the kitchen and returned with two bowls, milk and a box of cereal.

"There's more soufflé," Fawn protested.

"That's okay. I'm eating for two these days—and Andy's eating for about five, as usual," Lauren said. "We'll fill up on cereal."

Fawn's lips tightened, but she said nothing. C.J. caught her looking distastefully at the bright orange cardboard cereal box sitting on the lace tablecloth.

"So, what are you two doing today?" Lauren asked her brother.

"Well, I thought I could drive C.J. around a little, but it looks like it's going to be lousy out."

They all turned to the large windows that overlooked the lake. The water and sky were the same threatening shade of gray, and the leaves that still clung to the trees were rustling in the wind.

"It's going to snow," Andy commented. "They said on the weather last night that it would start around noon."

"You know what would be fun?" Lauren reached for the cereal box and filled her bowl again. "Scattergories."

"I love that game!" C.J. said.

"Why don't we all play? I'll go find it. It should be on that shelf in the family room." David started to get up.

"No, I don't think it's there anymore," Lauren said. "Dad, where are all our old games?"

Her father shrugged. "I'm not sure. Didn't you take them with you when you moved?"

"No."

Everyone looked at Fawn. She frowned. "Let's see...I think I remember moving some games about a year ago, when the decorators were here."

Lauren put down her spoon. "You didn't throw them away, did you?"

"No, of course not. They might be in the basement...or the attic. Try the attic. I think that's where everything from the family room went."

"Oh. So that's where our old yearbooks and family photo albums would be, too, then, right?" Lauren asked.

"Probably." Fawn looked uncomfortable. "Would anyone like more soufflé?"

Everyone murmured no.

The tension in the room made C.J. want to squirm. She looked at David. He was sipping his coffee and looked calm, as usual. So did his father.

But she was realizing, for the first time, the kind of strain his father's remarriage must have put on David. C.J. felt strange, thinking that she was going to be his wife, yet there were things about him that she didn't know.

Important things.

All of a sudden, looking at him, she thought that in some ways, he was almost a stranger.

"Roxie and I used to play up here when we were little," Lauren said, standing in the middle of the dusty attic floor and looking around.

"I always wished our house had an attic," C.J. said. "I wanted to be a girl detective, like Nancy Drew, and find secret maps and diaries under floorboards."

Lauren smiled at her. "Rox and I did that! We were always thumping on floors and walls up here, looking for hollow spaces."

"Did you ever find anything?"

"Nope. Just spiders."

C.J. cringed and looked to make sure there weren't any dangling over her head.

Lauren walked over to a stack of cardboard cartons by a dormer window. "I can't believe her," she said, shaking her head.

"Who?"

"Fawn."

"Oh."

"She has some nerve, dumping all our stuff up here. I mean, this was *our* house until she barged in and made it *hers*. When Mom was alive, things were so different, C.J. Did David ever tell you how she used to let us finger-paint at the kitchen table on rainy days?"

C.J. shook her head.

"And we had this big white refrigerator that was cov-ered—I mean *covered*—with stuff. Drawings I had made for Mom in grade school were still there when I went away to college. And clippings about Dad from the local paper, and pictures and recipes Mom wanted to try... She was always cooking or baking, even though she wasn't very good at it. Did David ever tell you about the birthday cake she made him when he was ten? She accidentally left out the sugar, and it was... yuck!" Lauren made a face and laughed.

"David never told me that," C.J. said. "In fact, he hardly ever talks about your mother."

"Yeah, well, I'm not surprised. Dave was never very talkative, anyway. And he was kind of a geek in junior high and high school, poor kid. But Mom always told him that he was the best, and that when he grew up, all the kids who had given him a hard time would want to be his friend. She tried so hard to give him confidence."

C.J. remembered feeling bad as a teenager when the kids at school had teased her mercilessly and called her Clara Cow. If only Lila had been supportive like David's mother had been. Lila's way of dealing with the situation had been to urge C.J. to lose weight so that people would stop mak-ing fun of her.

Lauren sighed. "Davey was really close to Mom—he was her little boy. When she got sick, he was the one who sat at her bedside for hours and hours while she slept. He would just look at her, and the expression on his face—" Lauren broke off and swallowed hard.

C.J. didn't know what to say. A lump was starting to edge its way up her own throat at the thought of poor David, a gawky teenager, sitting at his mother's deathbed. He'd never told her about that.

"And then," Lauren went on, "Mom died when my brother was about eighteen. I was away at college and Rox was married by then. But David was here with Dad. And one time, he told me that he would hear Dad crying every single night in his room."

"How terrible."

"Yeah. Mom and Dad really loved each other. He was so lonely and devastated when she died. Then Fawn came along, and I think he married her for companionship. It couldn't be love. He's so quiet with her. I mean, he was quiet with Mom, too, but in a different way. He always seemed content. Now he seems... I don't know, wistful."

"He still misses your mother," C.J. said softly, reaching up to press her finger against the inside corners of her eyes, so that tears wouldn't spill over.

"We all miss Mom. And now Fawn's here, trying to make our house this formal showplace. She got rid of all our old furniture. We used to have comfortable couches and this big, square, oak dining room table. The top of it was scarred and scratched, but Mom never put a tablecloth on it. We only ate in there on holidays, anyway. Now Fawn thinks we need to have these elaborate candlelight breakfasts. It just really makes me mad."

C.J. nodded. "David never told me any of that."

"Well, maybe he will, someday. But as I said, my brother likes to keep things inside." Lauren shoved her hair over her shoulder and looked again at the stack of boxes. "We'd better start looking for that game, or they're going to wonder what's happened to us. Here. You go through this box, and I'll check that one."

C.J. knelt on the uneven wooden floor and pulled the carton toward her. Inside, she found a stack of photo albums and some pictures in frames. Feeling as if she were snooping, she tried to dig through them quickly, just to make sure there were no games in the bottom of the box. But she couldn't help pausing to examine family photos in one of those matted frames that held collages of snapshots.

In most of the pictures, she saw a pretty, dark-haired woman whom she recognized as David's mother—he kept a framed photo of her in his apartment back in Chicago. She had lively brown eyes that were so much like David's, and the same wide, warm grin.

There was David in a posed school photo, his hair neatly parted on the side and one of his front teeth missing. And there he was again, looking older and awkward behind a drum set. She remembered that he'd told her he'd played in the school band as a teenager.

There were shots of his sisters, too. Lauren looked almost exactly the same, and Roxie was a taller, slightly chubby carbon copy of her.

"Did you find anything?" Lauren asked, and C.J. guiltily set the frame aside.

"Not really. Just some pictures."

"Oh, yeah? Let's see." Lauren crawled across the floor and peered over her shoulder. "Wow, here they are. These used to be hanging on the wall in the family room. Figures Fawn took them down. Look at this one."

She lifted a heavy wooden frame and C.J. saw that it was a black-and-white wedding photo of David's parents. They looked buoyant and in love.

"Your mom was so beautiful," C.J. said. "I love what she's wearing." It was a simple white dress with snug, elbow-length sleeves, a scoop neckline edged with a narrow band of lace and a plain skirt with a slight train.

"I know—I always loved that gown, too. It's still around here, someplace, packed away. I know Mom always wanted me or Roxie to wear it on our wedding days. But Rox and

Lou had a civil ceremony over in Germany. And I wanted to wear it when I got married, but it didn't fit. Mom was taller and more shapely than I am...when I'm not pregnant, that is. Normally, I'm straight up and down and flat as a board." She grinned at C.J. "I have to admit that it's nice to suddenly have boobs, you know?"

C.J. shrugged. "I don't know. I wish I had less there—and everywhere else."

"Why? You wouldn't want to be built like a twelve-year-old boy, like I am. Trust me. You know, you kind of remind me of my mom. The way you're built, and your coloring and everything."

"Maybe that's why David likes me. Isn't there some saying about that?"

"What—wanting a girl just like the girl that married dear old dad?" Lauren laughed. "I guess. So, what does your wedding gown look like?"

C.J. winced. "Sore subject."

"Why?"

"Because I haven't found one yet. Actually, I haven't even looked much. I hate everything I see in those magazines. They're all so frilly."

"Really?"

"Yup. I mean, when you've got natural padding, like I do, you don't want a huge dress that will add fifty pounds. I wish I could find something like this," C.J. said, pointing to David's mother's wedding dress in the picture. "This is exactly like what I would want to wear."

Lauren grabbed her arm excitedly. "Then why don't you?"

"What?"

"Wear my mother's dress? It's still here. Let's find it and you can try it on."

"Oh, Lauren, I wasn't hinting—I mean, I couldn't do that."

"Sure you could. It would mean so much, C.J. Mom always wanted someone to wear it, and I think it would be really special if it were David's bride. Unless, of course, you don't want to wear a used dress—"

"No, of course that's not it. I'd just feel kind of funny taking the dress. What if it bothers your dad? Or Fawn? Or David?"

"Are you kidding? Dad would be so happy. And Fawn— well, who cares what she thinks? I know David would be really touched, and that's what counts, right?" Lauren stood and started across the attic toward an old wooden wardrobe in one corner. "I'm pretty sure it's hanging in there."

C.J. followed her, feeling a tiny flicker of excitement. She *did* love the dress, and it would solve her problem.

Still... What if it had disintegrated or something? What if it was stained or in tatters after all these years?

But it wasn't. When Lauren found the right garment bag and unzipped it to reveal the long white dress, C.J. saw that it looked perfect. The rich fabric was pure, heavy silk, and it had mellowed to a shade that reminded C.J. of gourmet French vanilla ice cream.

"It's beautiful," C.J. said, tentatively reaching out to stroke the dress with her fingertips. "I absolutely love it."

"Go ahead, try it on," Lauren urged. "I can't wait to see you in it."

C.J. hesitated, not wanting to take off her clothes right here in the middle of the room. She had never been thrilled about baring her body in front of anyone.

As if she'd suddenly realized what was holding C.J. back, Lauren said, "Oh, you can go over into that corner by the window to change. I think there's an old cheval mirror back there someplace, too. I'll keep looking for the game. Call me if you need help getting the dress on."

"Okay. Thanks."

C.J. gently lifted the hanger from the bag and carried the dress over to the corner, careful not to let the skirt drag on the floor.

She glanced out the window and saw that it had started snowing. Soft feathery flakes drifted lazily past the streaked glass. It was the wet kind of snow that would coat the trees and turn the world into a wonderland. Maybe she and David could take a walk in it later. The thought sent happy little shivers through her.

She turned back to the dress.

What if it didn't fit? What if it was too tight or too short? There was only one way to find out.

She swiftly took off her leggings and sweater and stepped into the gown. Carefully she pulled it up and slipped her arms into the sleeves. So far, it felt just right.

She reached back and realized that the long row of round fabric buttons on the back were actually meant to be fastened. Hmm. On the "frocks" C.J. had tried on that day at Weissman's, there was always a zipper underneath the buttons.

"Um, Lauren?" she asked, after it had taken her nearly five minutes to hook the first few buttons. "Can you help me?"

David's sister was beside her within seconds. "Oh, C.J.," she said excitedly. "This is gorgeous on you. Here, turn around."

C.J. tried to stand patiently as Lauren worked her way up the back of the dress. The fabric wasn't straining to meet over her hips and bust. That was a good sign.

Finally the last button was snug in its loop, and Lauren said, "Okay, let's look in the mirror."

The moment C.J. glimpsed her full-length reflection in the old cheval mirror, she made up her mind.

The dress was perfect. *Perfect.* It showed off curves, not bulges. The muted ivory fabric made her skin look creamy and soft.

"Well?" Lauren asked, stepping back and pressing her knuckles against her mouth as she waited for C.J.'s reaction.

"I'd love to wear it, Lauren," she said, shaking her head in wonder at herself in the mirror. "I can't believe it. This is exactly what I always pictured."

"I'm so glad!" Lauren stepped forward and gave her a hug. "You're going to be a beautiful bride, C.J."

And for the first time, C.J. dared to let herself believe that.

"Well?" David asked, as the Fasten Seat Belt sign *dinged* and turned off. He settled back in his seat. "What did you think?"

"Of what?" C.J. turned from the window now that there was nothing to see. Moments ago, Buffalo had been all lit up and twinkling below them as they took off, but now the snowy landscape was obscured by a thick layer of clouds.

"Of everything," David told her. "The weekend, my family, the town, whatever."

She smiled at his anxious expression and reached out to squeeze his hand. "The weekend was a lot of fun. I loved getting to know your family—they made me feel like a part of everything. And the town was beautiful—especially blanketed in snow."

"Yeah, well October's a little early for a storm like the one we got, but at least it cleared up today so that we could fly out of here. I can't tell you how many times I've had trouble getting into or out of the Buffalo airport."

"I hope everyone can manage to get to our wedding," C.J. said. "I mean, in December, the weather's going to be so unpredictable."

"Don't worry."

"You always say that, David. Don't you ever worry about anything?"

"Not things I can't control." He shrugged and reached for the USAir magazine in the seat pocket in front of him.

C.J. put out a hand to stop him. "Wait, David, don't read."

"Why not?"

"Don't you want to talk to me instead? We haven't been alone together all weekend."

"Oh. Sure." He sat back. "What do you want to talk about?"

"I don't know. Tell me about what it was like growing up in that big old house."

"It was... you know. It was nice."

"Lauren said you guys used to have a tree house out back."

"Yeah."

"She said your mother helped you build it."

"Uh-huh." He looked past her, out the window.

"She said your mother used to love to work with wood and a hammer and nails. That's so interesting. I mean, most people's *fathers* help them with tree houses or doghouses or whatever. I can't see *my* mother building anything. Your mom sounds great."

"Yup. She was. Here comes the flight attendant. Do you want something to drink?"

"I guess."

C.J. watched David turn the latch in front of him and lower his tray table. He looked at her expectantly.

She sighed and lowered her own. The flight attendant was still a few rows ahead of them.

"David?" she asked.

"Mmm-hmm?"

"Why don't you like to tell me about certain things?"

Wait—that hadn't come out right. She immediately realized her question had put him on the defensive when she saw the way his jaw had tightened.

"What's that supposed to mean?" he asked, folding his arms.

"I mean, how come there are some things you don't want to share with me? Like about your past—losing your mother, and your father marrying Fawn..." She trailed off, wishing she hadn't brought any of this up.

He refused to look at her. "I don't know what you mean."

"Never mind." She watched as the flight attendant handed the couple in front of them two steaming cups of coffee, then opened a can of soda for the man across the aisle.

David was silent beside her, closed off in a way that was all too familiar to C.J. This was how he'd acted last year when she'd been trying to get him to make a commitment, or at least to talk about how he felt about her.

She probably should just accept that David wasn't someone who easily talked about his feelings—especially difficult or unhappy ones. But there was a side of her that resented the way he closed off parts of himself, refusing to trust her by revealing his whole self.

Oh, there were times when he was honest with her, when he shared painful stories about his past. Like on their second date, when he had told her about how some bitchy, popular girl—Amanda Billings, C.J. recalled—had stood him up and humiliated him.

But that was a rare occasion. He usually didn't talk about things like that, and he never discussed losing his mother.

C.J., on the other hand, had told him every detail about her own painful childhood—about the horrible "Clara Cow" nickname, and how she'd never really had a boyfriend and how she'd lost her virginity to some guy she had met at a concert and barely knew.

Then again, she kept things from him, too.

Like the thing that had happened with Dig.

But that was different. That was something that would drive her and David apart, not bring them closer.

On the other hand, maybe not. Maybe keeping that from him was a mistake. Maybe they shouldn't hide things from each other in their marriage. Maybe they shouldn't let secrets build walls between them. Didn't they owe it to each other to be entirely honest and open about everything?

Wasn't that what marriage was all about?

"David?" C.J. asked, turning to him.

"Yeah?"

Just then, the flight attendant stepped in front of their row and asked cheerfully, "What can I get for you two tonight?"

"I'll have a Coke," David said.

"Diet Coke," C.J. said.

By the time their drinks and small foil packets of peanuts were in front of them, she'd changed her mind about spilling her guts or demanding that David spill his.

It would just have to wait.

Six

Rabbi Sam Krantz was a short, balding man with pale blue eyes and a beard. He greeted C.J. and David at the door to his study with a pleasant smile.

"Come in, come in," he said, ushering them to a nubby wheat-colored couch. "Have a seat. Rachel, will you please close the door behind us?" he asked over his shoulder.

The soft-spoken woman who had delivered C.J. and David to the study said, "Certainly, Rabbi," and shut the three of them in the study with a quiet click.

"Tell me about yourselves," was the first thing Rabbi Krantz said after settling himself in a chair opposite them.

C.J. blinked. What did the man want to know? Hobbies? The last book she had read? How they had met?

She looked at David, who appeared calm, as usual. He said easily, "What kind of information do you need, Rabbi?"

"Let's start with the basics. Why do you want to get married?"

C.J. raised her eyebrows.

Wasn't that obvious? Why did anyone want to get married?

Even David seemed a little taken aback. *"Why?"* he repeated, turning to C.J. He seemed to think it was her turn to respond.

Gee, thanks a lot, honey, she thought, and cleared her throat. "We, uh, we want to get married because we want to be together forever."

"That's right," David said.

"But you could do that without being married, couldn't you?" The rabbi's blue eyes were intent. "These days, you could just live together, couldn't you?"

Boy, you wouldn't catch Father Manelli saying something like that, C.J. thought, glancing at David.

"I guess we *could,*" he told the rabbi, "but that wouldn't be enough. We love each other, and we want to be a family."

Wow.

Hearing David put it that way sent chills through C.J. He had never said anything like that to her before.

We want to be a family.

Wow. How sweet.

I really, really love you, David Griffin, C.J. thought, staring at him.

Apparently, the rabbi was pleased, too, because he said warmly, "That's what I was looking for. You love each other."

C.J. and David exchanged a happy nod that said *Yes, we sure do.*

"Here's my next question," the rabbi went on, leaning forward. "Given your different faiths, why do you want to go to all the trouble of having a religious ceremony? Clara Joy?"

Her immediate impulse was to say, *Don't ask me. I'm not the one who's insisting on it.* But that probably wouldn't be prudent under the circumstances. The rabbi might decide he didn't want to deal with a bride who had ambivalent feelings about religion.

On the other hand, what could she say? This was David's idea. Why was *she* the one who was put on the spot?

She thought wildly before something popped into her head and spilled off her tongue. "David and I feel that God has blessed us in giving us each other, so it wouldn't feel right not to have Him present at our wedding ceremony."

Rabbi Krantz beamed.

So did David. "That's exactly right," he said, nodding.

"Splendid," the rabbi said.

Part of C.J. was noticing the word *splendid*—something you hardly ever heard these days unless you hung out with your grandparents. The rest of her was wondering what David would have answered if the rabbi had asked for *his* reasons for wanting a religious ceremony.

And once again, she felt vaguely frustrated. What was going on in that level head of David's? And why didn't she know?

Why did it seem, lately, as though there were so many things about him that she didn't know?

You know that he loves you and he wants to be a family with you. Isn't that enough?

It should be ... shouldn't it?

She heard her name and turned her attention back to the conversation.

"You'll be glad to know, Clara Joy, that I've spoken to several priests," Rabbi Sam was saying. "Unfortunately, they're all booked for the Saturday you're getting married. However, I'll keep trying to find someone for you. David mentioned that your own priest wasn't very helpful?"

"Not exactly," C.J. admitted reluctantly, suddenly feeling defensive even though Father Manelli wasn't exactly her favorite person in the world. "But he did give us his blessing. He's just a little ... old-fashioned."

The rabbi nodded. "Well, I'll keep checking around for a priest. Now, why don't you tell me more about yourselves? How did you meet?"

"It was a blind date," David said promptly.

And as he launched into the story of how his stepmother and Lila Clarke had fixed them up, C.J. let her thoughts wander back to David and all the things she didn't know about him. And what about the things he didn't know about her?

What about that one thing in particular?

That *Dig Lawrence* thing.

What would he say if she told him? Would he call off the wedding? Was that enough of a reason not to get married—finding out that your fiancée had cheated on you over a year ago, before she even *was* your fiancée?

Of course it wasn't.

Was it?

David wouldn't call off the wedding, C.J. told herself. *He loves you. He wants to be a family with you. That's all you need to focus on.*

"Okay, how about that pattern, then?" C.J. asked David, pointing to a Royal Doulton place setting next to the Wedgwood one he'd just dissed.

David peered at the engraved card in front of it. " 'Old Country Roses'?" He shook his head. "Nah."

C.J. clenched her jaw and glanced at Darla Garliche, the chubby middle-aged blonde from Marshall Field's Bridal Registry service, who was standing by with her clipboard. Her blue eyes looked suspiciously vacant—definitely more bored than sympathetic.

C.J. decided that maybe she and David weren't the only engaged couple who couldn't agree on a china pattern. But they didn't have much time to spare. And at this rate, they'd be lucky if they were finished registering in time to walk down the aisle.

C.J. sighed and cast a longing glance at the beautiful Royal Doulton setting, then looked grimly at her fiancé.

He looked apologetic…sort of. "Sorry, C.J., but I can't help it. I just had something a little less…dainty in mind."

"Dainty? This pattern is *not* dainty." C.J. looked to Darla Garliche for backup.

The woman was completely focused on peeling away a hangnail on her pinkie. Nice.

Rolling her eyes, C.J. turned back to David. "I mean, look at this plate. The flowers are bright. They're splashy. They're not dainty."

He shrugged. "I'm a guy, C.J. All flowers look dainty."

Darla Garliche raised her head and cracked a smile at that. Then she actually offered a suggestion. "Why don't we walk around to the other side? The patterns there are a little more basic and masculine."

"Good idea," David said, putting his hand under C.J.'s elbow to guide her.

Basic and masculine? C.J. was thinking. *Great. Just great.*

They arrived in front of the display. The patterns were mostly stark white and rimmed with bold geometric patterns in primary colors or black.

C.J. didn't have to look twice to know she hated them all.

"Hey, this is more like it," David said cheerfully. "Look at that dish, C.J. Just a simple black band around the edge. What do you think?"

"I think black bands are for funerals," she said darkly.

David grinned. "I guess it's out of the question, then, huh?"

"Definitely."

"Ouch," said Darla Garliche, sticking her pinkie into her mouth.

David pointed to another pattern. "Okay, what about that one, then?"

C.J. looked. Maroon triangles on a cream-colored background. "No way."

"That one?" Navy stripes on hunter green.

"I hate it."

Darla Garliche said, "Excuse me, but I'll be right back. I'm bleeding." She waved her wounded pinkie at them, then stuck it back into her mouth and wandered away.

C.J. looked at David. They both cracked up.

Then C.J. sobered and glanced back at the china display. "David, what are we going to do? I hate everything you like, and you hate everything I like. If we can't manage to pick out a china pattern, how are we going to make major decisions together?"

"We'll manage. We've come this far, haven't we?" He grabbed her fingers and squeezed.

"Yes. But now that we're into the nitty gritty..." She shrugged.

"Okay, look," David said. "We can't drag this out all day. I'm starving. Let's skip the china for now and pick out everything else. Then we can go have lunch upstairs. I already know what I want. Chicken pot pie."

That was the specialty of Marshall Field's Walnut Room, and C.J.'s mouth watered at the thought of it. But there would be no chicken pot pie for her today. She hadn't lost an ounce in the two weeks since they'd been back from Buffalo. Now she had about eight weeks to lose around forty pounds—and then have David's mother's dress altered to fit her.

Lauren had shipped it to her last week, and it was now hanging in the back of her closet. C.J. hadn't told David yet that she was going to wear his mother's wedding gown, and she'd sworn his sister to secrecy.

C.J. couldn't help feeling a little funny about it, as though she were intruding on something he considered very private. What if he was upset when he found out? She had no idea how he'd react, which bothered her more than anything else.

A few times, C.J. had actually decided that she shouldn't wear the dress after all, that she should just forget about it and find something else. But then she would go to her closet, open the garment bag and caress the rich silk fabric. And she would again know that it was the perfect wedding dress, and she *had* to wear it—and that was that.

"So, do you agree with me?" David asked her, tugging on her hand.

"About what?"

"That we should forget the china for now and move on?"

"But, David, we need china."

"Why?"

"Everyone does. It's just…it's what you do when you get married. You register so that people can buy you wedding gifts."

Not, thank heaven, shower gifts. Lila Clarke had wanted to throw her a bridal shower, but C.J. absolutely refused. She had enough to worry about between now and the wedding. Her mother had backed down without *too* much of an argument, which was unlike her. C.J. dared to hope that maybe now that she was going to be a married woman, her mother might finally be mellowing a little.

"Fine," David was saying. "So let's register. But not for china. There are a lot of other things we need. Things that are way more important."

"Like what?" C.J. asked warily.

"Like tools. You know Kent, that guy from work who I was telling you about? The one who just got married? Well, he and his wife registered at a hardware store, and they got—"

"A hardware store?" C.J. looked at him in horror. "David, there is no way we're going to—"

"I know, but I was just pointing out that there are things we're going to need that will come in more handy than plates will."

"Oh, really? You don't plan to eat three meals a day for the rest of our lives?"

"It's no big deal. We'll go to Wal-Mart and pick up some stuff," he said casually. "We don't need fancy expensive dishes for everyday."

He had a point. Still, every bride knew that part of the excitement of getting married was picking out your china pattern, something you would have throughout your life together.

"David, if we don't get china now, we never will."

"Sure we will."

"How? That will never be a priority in the future."

He shrugged and asked calmly, "Then why should it be now?"

C.J. was exasperated. "I can't believe you don't under-stand why this is important."

"I can't believe you'd rather get expensive plates that we'll never use instead of stuff that we'll use all the time."

"Like what?"

"Like a blender. Or a vacuum cleaner."

"I don't want to register for a vacuum cleaner. That, we can get at Wal-Mart."

"And how about that sandwich-making machine I saw in the appliance department on the way in? We can't get one of those at Wal-Mart."

"A sandwich maker? And how is that a necessity?"

It was David's turn to look exasperated. But before he could respond, the battle-scarred Darla Garliche reap-peared, the tip of her pinkie swathed in a white gauze bandage.

"How are we doing?" she asked optimistically, patting her tight blond bun with her good hand. "Did we select our china pattern?"

C.J. and David exchanged a glance. She sighed and waved her hand, motioning for David to do whatever he wanted.

"We've decided to concentrate on other things for the time being," David told the woman.

"All right. That sounds like a wise idea."

David shot C.J. a look that said, *Sandwich maker, here we come!*

Darla Garliche consulted the registry list that was at-tached to her clipboard. "All right, follow me. You can pick out your silver pattern next, and then we'll head for crystal stemware."

"Hello?" C.J. asked in a rush, grabbing the phone with one hand while pulling a clunky but comfortable work sneaker onto her left foot with the other.

"Hello, is this Clara Joy Clarke?"

"Yes," she said impatiently, glancing at the clock. It was just about six o'clock, which meant that she had two minutes to get out the door. She hurriedly wedged the phone between her shoulder and ear so she could use both hands to tie her shoe, and asked, "Who is this?"

"My name is is Barnabas Myer, and I'm—"

The phone slipped and fell, landing squarely on her shoeless right foot.

"Owww...dammit!" C.J. grabbed it and rubbed her toes, even more annoyed with—had he said his name was *Barnabas?*

She jerked the phone back up to her ear.

"Clara Joy?" the voice was asking tentatively. "Hello?"

"Sorry about that," she said curtly.

"Thought you hung up on me." He chuckled.

She didn't have time to chuckle back. She looked at the clock again and said, "Look, I'm late for work, and—"

"Oh, I'm sorry. I assumed this would be a good time to call. I thought you might be just getting *home* from work. What is it that you do?"

"I'm a bartender." She shoved her sore right foot into her other shoe.

"Huh. Interesting. Well, let me get right to the point. Rabbi Krantz over at the Temple Beth Emmanuel contacted me about your wedding, and when I said I was available, he suggested that I call you directly."

"He..." C.J. stopped tying her shoelace and frowned. What was going on?

Was this—oh, Lord, was this man a priest?

I cursed when I dropped the phone. I told him I'm a bartender.

"Clara Joy?"

"Uh . . . are you a priest?"

"Yup."

He didn't sound like a priest, though. He sounded so casual and . . . young.

And he'd just said *yup.*

"I'm sorry, Father. I didn't realize . . ."

He chuckled again. "No big deal."

No big deal?

What kind of priest was this, anyway?

"Listen, obviously this is a bad time, Clara Joy. Why don't you get going to work, and give me a call tomorrow at the rectory. Do you have a pen around?"

"I, uh . . . I have to go find one. Can you hang—"

"No, don't do that. You don't have time. Look, it's simple. Just call St. Clotilda's here in Wheaton—you can get the number from Information—and ask for me, Father Barney."

"St. . . . *Clotilda's?*" C.J. repeated. She was thinking, Father *Barney?*

"You got it. Take care, and I'll talk to you tomorrow."

"Okay . . ."

"Great. See ya," he said, and there was a click.

C.J. hung up, grabbed her coat and keys and headed for the door.

Father *Barney*.

Hmm . . .

Maybe there was hope for her wedding after all.

"Hi, Em—ooh, he's gotten so big!" C.J. said in a hushed voice as her friend Emily Granger answered the door with her sleepy baby in her arms.

"He's definitely much heavier than he was when you saw him at the christening in July," Emily whispered. She stepped back to let C.J. in. "I'm going to go put him down for his nap, and then we can chat. Go ahead and have a seat—the living room is through there."

C.J. nodded and headed through the archway as Emily carried the baby up the carved wooden staircase.

In the living room, the first thing C.J. noticed was a large framed wedding portrait on the opposite wall, above the fireplace. In it, Emily and her husband, Marsh, were looking dreamily into each other's eyes.

C.J. stepped closer to examine it. How happy and young they looked! So different from now. . . .

The Grangers had just gotten back together after being separated for several months. They had reconciled when their son was born in June. The only time C.J. had seen them since was in July, at the baby's christening. Both Emily and Marsh had looked tired and strained that day.

David had told C.J. it was probably from the stress of new parenthood, but C.J. wasn't so sure. Emily had *said* she was happy to be back with her husband, but maybe she wasn't really....

On the other hand, the living room was filled with evidence of a happy family life—framed photos of the Grangers and their newborn on the mantel, an embroidered poem about love on the wall, a row of photo albums on the bookshelf.

And the furniture had an expensive aura about it, giving the room an air of permanence that was lacking in C.J.'s mix-and-match apartment. Seamus's taste ran to chrome and black lacquer, and hers to lace curtains and Laura Ashley print fabrics.

C.J. wondered how soon she and David would be able to afford a large, comfortable house like this one the Grangers had just bought in Wilmette. Like David, Marsh Granger was in banking. Of course, both Emily and Marsh came from moneyed families on Long Island, which didn't hurt. And Emily had confided to C.J. that her parents had been so happy when she and Marsh reconciled that they had offered to help them buy the house.

"So how are your wedding plans coming along?" Emily asked, coming into the living room behind C.J.

"Don't ask."

"Uh-oh. Sounds ominous."

"Actually, it was ominous until the other day. But now that Father Barney's on board..." She trailed off and waited for Emily's reaction.

"Father *Barney*? As in ... Barney?"

"As in *Barnabas,* who was actually a saint, according to Seamus, who always somehow knows about that kind of stuff. I guess it's all those years of Catholic school. Anyway, the rabbi David had found put us in touch with this guy. He seems really cool, Emily, believe it or not. I mean, he's no Father Manelli.''

"Father Manelli?"

"The priest in my hometown church. I talked to this Father Barney over the phone the other day, and he said he's done, like, a million interfaith ceremonies, which is a good sign. And he's really young, still in his twenties—and cool, if you can believe that. I mean, we were talking about music and stuff.... He likes Mercury Rev.''

"*Who?*"

"That's what I expected *him* to say. They're my favorite band. David's, too.''

"And Father Barney's, too?" Emily looked incredulous.

"No, actually, he's more into Smashing Pumpkins.''

"Oh.''

"So I feel much better now about everything," C.J. said. "I mean, I really liked him. David and I are going to meet him in person next week.''

"See? I told you everything would work out," Emily told her, walking over to straighten a framed Degas print on the wall.

"Yeah, and you were right as usual." C.J. thought her friend seemed distracted. "You know, this room is gorgeous, Emily. I love the hardwood floors. They must be impossible to keep polished, though.''

"Actually, Marsh insisted on hiring someone to come in once a week to clean. I've just been so exhausted lately, with the baby and everything....'' She flopped into a costly-looking floral chintz-covered chair. '' Mind if I just sit for a minute? I only got an hour's sleep last night.''

"You poor thing." C.J. noticed the deep trenches under Emily's eyes. She looked pale and drained. "Why couldn't you sleep?''

For some reason, she half expected Emily to say that the strain of living with Marsh again was keeping her up nights.

But the answer was, "Joseph. He's teething, and he's miserable. Marsh has been really good about it, though. He gets up every time the baby makes a sound. He tells me to go back to sleep, but I just can't lie in bed while Joseph is screaming."

"It must be hard."

"It is." Emily yawned. "How about some tea? I could use a shot of caffeine, and now that I'm not breast-feeding anymore, I'm allowed again, thank God."

"Let me go make it. You stay here."

"Don't be ridiculous, C.J. Do you know how nice it is to have some company on a weekday afternoon? I'm usually so lonely, isolated out here in suburban baby-land with no one to talk to."

"I know what you mean. Too bad you didn't live closer to me. Everyone I know works nine-to-five. I don't know what to do with myself during the days."

"I thought you said you loved the freedom," Emily commented as she led the way through a formal dining room.

"I did. I mean, I *do*. But after the wedding, I need to figure out what I want to do about my career."

Emily stopped in front of an ornately carved dark wood china cabinet and opened a glass-paned door. "You mean, going back into television production?"

"Maybe. Or maybe something else. Right now, I feel like I'm in limbo."

"You and me both." Emily took two delicate cups and saucers from the cabinet, closed the door and continued toward the back of the house with C.J. right behind her.

"*You* feel like you're in limbo, Em? But I thought you'd made up your mind to become a fashion designer." Emily had been a teacher before the separation with Marsh. "I thought you said you were going to start back at the design school after the holidays."

"I am going to. That's not what I meant about being in limbo." Emily led the way into a spacious, modern kitchen, set the cups and saucers on the counter and went straight to the stove. She moved a copper teakettle to the front burner and turned it on high, then turned around to look C.J. in the eye. "I meant me and Marsh."

"Oh." C.J. shifted her weight and wondered what to say. "You mean, your marriage is in limbo?"

Emily nodded.

"But I thought everything was fine. I mean, you guys are together again, and you bought the house and you have the baby...."

"Right. But we sleep in separate rooms, C.J. And if it weren't for the baby, I don't know where we'd be right now, in terms of *us*. Our relationship. Probably in divorce court, like we'd planned before Joseph came along."

C.J. didn't know what to say.

Emily winced and reached up and rubbed the spot between her neck and her shoulder. She went over and settled heavily in a chair at the table in front of three paned windows that looked out over a sweeping yard.

C.J. walked over, sat across from her and asked, "What happened to you guys, Emily?"

"I have no idea," her friend said, still gazing out the window. "I thought I knew Marsh inside and out. You know our story—I mean, we'd been together since we were teenagers. We grew up together, really. And then one day, it was like I woke up and found myself married to a stranger."

Her words caused something to lurch in the pit of C.J.'s stomach. "What do you mean?" she asked in a hollow voice.

"I mean, there were so many things he didn't know about me. Things he didn't understand. And things I didn't know about him, either. In all those months that we lived apart, before the baby was born, I missed him so much, C.J. He'd been a part of my life for so long, and it just didn't seem right to be without him. But now that we're back together, I have that same feeling again. That I don't really *know* him. I look at him, and I have no idea what he's thinking, what he wants, how he feels. It's horrible.''

C.J. stared into Emily's tear-rimmed eyes numbly. She knew she should be trying to comfort her friend, or help her, but all she could think about was that she herself was about to marry a man who sometimes seemed like a stranger. How well did she really know David?

What made her think that she and David could make it together, could stay together forever? Emily and Marsh Granger had known each other far longer than she and David had, and look at what was happening to them.

Look at Kyle and Tammy.

And Christopher and Madelyn.

And even Jessica and Jake, who had been cooing contentedly at each other only a few months ago, were having problems these days.

It suddenly seemed to C.J. that she and David were utter fools to think that their marriage had a remote chance of lasting.

The teakettle started rattling on the stove, and its low hum rapidly grew into an ear-splitting whistle.

Emily jumped up and dashed over to move it off the burner, then stood with her head cocked, as though listening for something. After a moment she said, ''Thank goodness that didn't wake the baby. I want him to sleep. Actually, I *need* him to sleep—I need a break.''

C.J. joined her at the counter and watched as she settled an Earl Gray tea bag into each of the cups. Emily poured hot water into both, then handed one, balanced carefully on its saucer, to C.J.

''Why don't we go back into the living room? It's more comfortable,'' Emily suggested.

''Good idea. You need to relax.'' C.J. followed her back through the house, and they both settled on the floral chintz couch.

For a few moments, the only sound in the room was the ticking of the mantel clock. Emily seemed lost in sad thoughts.

C.J. tried to think of something to say. She sipped her tea, noticing the pretty pink rosebud pattern on the dainty, gold-rimmed cup.

"This is beautiful china, Emily," she said.

"Thanks." Her friend smiled briefly. "It's our wedding china."

"Really? David and I went to register last week at Marshall Field's."

She decided she didn't feel like going into the whole story of how they hadn't been able to choose china, silver or crystal, and in the end, registered only for simple, everyday Pfaltzgraff, stainless-steel and glass. She just wanted to forget all about that frustrating episode.

Emily's face clouded, and there was a faraway look in her eyes. "I remember when Marsh and I went to register for china before we got married," she said. "We just couldn't agree. Finally he gave in—but not without a battle. And he still sulks about how much he hates this pattern."

The knot in C.J.'s stomach tightened.

Emily shook her head. "I'll never forget what it was like that day at Saks. Totally frustrating. Everything I loved, Marsh hated, and vice versa. I should have realized back then that it wasn't a good sign."

C.J. didn't say anything to that. She couldn't.

She just stared down at the rosebud-patterned cup in her hand as a sick feeling stole over her.

Seven

Mr. and Mrs. Thomas Clarke
and
Mr. and Mrs. Robert Griffin
invite you to share in the joy
at the marriage of their children
Clara Joy
and
David
on Saturday, the thirtieth of December
at half past one in the afternoon
The Moose Lodge
Green Hollow Road
Oak Hills, Illinois

"I don't believe her," C.J. muttered, staring at the invitation she had just taken from the box her mother had mailed her.

"You don't believe who?" David asked. He was standing behind her, reading over her shoulder.

"Who else? My mother! She had them put 'Clara Joy' on this!"

"She wasn't supposed to?"

"No! Oh, God, I don't believe this," she wailed, staring at the embossed black printing on the creamy white card. "This is why I didn't want my mother to place the order, David. Why did I listen to her? We should have done it through that stationery place here in the city, like I wanted to in the first place."

"You know why we let her do it. She knows the guy who owns the printing place in your hometown. He gave us a big discount, remember?"

"I *know* why we let her do it, David. But when I wrote out the wording, it said 'C.J.' She changed it, even though I warned her not to."

"Hey, it's okay," David said, slipping his arms around her from behind and resting his chin on her head. "The invitations look beautiful. And so does your name."

"But I hate 'Clara Joy'!"

Oh, Lord, she was crying.

And once the tears started spilling over, she let them keep coming, splattering drop by drop onto the wedding invitation in her hand.

"David, you *know* I hate 'Clara Joy.'"

"I know."

"It reminds me of when everyone in school used to call me 'Clara Cow,'" she wept miserably.

"Shh...I know." David turned her around and pulled her against him so that her wet face was pressed against his chest. "Come on. Stop crying now, okay? It'll be all right."

"No, it won't." She clung to him, crying so hard, she was quaking.

"Sure, it will. We'll have the invitations reprinted."

"We can't do that. They have to be mailed out tomorrow. It's too late."

He didn't say anything. He obviously knew she was right. They had been waiting for the invitations to come in for the past two weeks. When Lila had called yesterday to say they had finally arrived, C.J. had told her to send them by overnight courier. Lila, of course, had offered to address them and send them out from there, but C.J. wasn't taking any chances. Knowing her mother, she'd slip invitations to the relatives C.J. had cut from the list to make room for her and David's friends.

For a few minutes, C.J. kept crying, and David kept stroking her hair in silence.

Then he said, "Come on, C.J., pull yourself together. It's no use getting all upset over something you can't do anything about."

She was sobbing too hard to even answer him. How could she tell him that it wasn't just the invitations that were upsetting her? How could she say that for the past two weeks, ever since that day at Emily's, she had been terrified that they were making a big mistake? She'd kept her misgivings inside, had tried to push them away and pretend they didn't exist.

And now every ounce of pent-up anguish was gushing out in a miserable torrent.

And David, poor bewildered David, had no idea why she was *really* crying.

The worst part was, she loved him so very, very much.

And she knew he loved her.

But love wasn't going to be enough to make their marriage last. Emily had told C.J. that she loved Marsh, that she always had. And now look at them.

What if one day, C.J. and David woke up in separate bedrooms, with a wall of misunderstandings and bitterness lying between them?

There was no guarantee that it wouldn't happen.

Look at them now, before they were even married. Here she was, keeping a huge secret from David. And obviously he was keeping things from her.

There were so many times, especially lately, when she'd look at his placid face and wonder what was going on in his mind. She wanted so much for him to open up to her about his feelings, but she hadn't even tried to draw him out lately. It only made him close himself off from her even more.

If they didn't trust each other enough to share everything about themselves now, what was going to happen later?

"Hello. Is Christopher there?" C.J. asked into the telephone later that night.

"Hang on a second," said the guy who had answered on the other end. "Yo, Chris! Phone for you." There was a clattering sound in her ear, as if he'd dropped the phone.

While she waited, C.J. looked at David, who was sitting on the floor in front of the coffee table, addressing an envelope. He glanced up at her as he licked the flap, and smiled. She smiled back, and he went back to what he was doing, relieved, obviously, that she'd snapped out of her crying jag.

Luckily, she'd managed to pull herself together, telling herself that she was just exhausted, that was all. Her wedding was going to be fine and her marriage was going to be fine and that was that.

"Yeah, this is Chris," said a familiar voice in her ear.

"Hi!"

"Hi . . . who is this?"

"A voice from your past," C.J. told him.

"Uh-oh. Is this Miss Crabtree, my old kindergarten teacher?" he asked, and C.J. could hear the grin in his voice.

"No one in real life has a teacher named Miss Crabtree, Chris," C.J. said, laughing. "And anyway, I'm not from *that* far in the past."

"I know this voice! C. J. Clarke—how the hell have you been?"

"Fine. How's New York?"

"It's great. How are the wedding plans coming along?"

"Actually, that's kind of why I'm calling you. I need your address so I can send you an invitation."

"Cool. When's the wedding, again?"

"The Saturday after Christmas."

"Jeez, I hope I can make it."

"Won't you be coming home to spend the holidays with Madelyn . . . or your dad?" she tacked on hurriedly, wondering if bringing Madelyn up was such a good idea.

"Actually, I'm coming back to Chicago in two weeks to surprise Madelyn for Thanksgiving," he said, and his voice sounded a little wistful, as if he missed her.

C.J. smiled. That was a good sign.

"But I'm not sure how much time I'll have at Christmas," he went on. "We're going to be in the middle of recording our new album by then."

"Sounds exciting."

"But I promise I'll do my best to get there for your wedding," Chris said.

They chatted for a few more minutes. Then he gave her his new address, and they hung up, promising to try to get together when he was in town.

"How is he?" David asked, glancing up from the envelope he was addressing.

"He sounds good. I guess he and Madelyn are still trying to work things out. He's coming home for Thanksgiving to be with her."

"Good."

"You don't sound surprised."

"I'm not."

"You're not? I am. I thought they were finished."

"Nah. Chris loves her."

"How do you know?"

"I'm a guy. A guy knows about another guy," he said simply, and went back to copying an address off the list in front of him.

C.J. thought about how Chris had told her a few months ago that he wasn't ready to settle down with Madelyn. Maybe he'd underestimated himself. Maybe now that they were apart, he realized that he couldn't live without her.

C.J. went back over to the coffee table and sat down next to David. She leaned over and kissed his cheek, then picked up her pen and reached for another invitation.

C.J. came home from work at one-thirty in the morning to find Seamus sitting in the living room. The bluish flicker of the television and the glowing tip of his cigarette were the only lights in the room.

"What are you doing?" she asked, kicking off her sneakers and flopping down next to him. "Where's Chad?"

"Watching *Key Largo*, and he's in my room, sleeping. Look at Humphrey Bogart," he said, gesturing toward the black and white image on the screen. "The man is a rock."

C.J. nodded.

Seamus shook his head. "He died of cancer when he was still in his fifties. He was strong until the end, you know? He went out the way he lived his life."

"Mmm-hmm," C.J. murmured.

Normally it was so easy to forget that Seamus was HIV positive. But at times like this, when he talked about death and looked tired and sad, the truth hit her full force.

She couldn't say anything else for a minute. An enormous lump had filled her throat, and she hoped he wouldn't look at her and see the tears that were seeping into her eyes.

She swallowed hard and reached for the pack of cigarettes on the coffee table. Once in a while, she smoked one or two cigarettes—but only when David wasn't around. He abhorred smoking and C.J. had a feeling he wouldn't be thrilled to see her doing it.

Seamus, his gaze still riveted on the television, silently passed her his lighter.

She flicked it and held the flame against the cigarette and drew the smoke deeply into her lungs. She held it there, then exhaled a thin gray stream and imagined all her anxiety about Seamus and David and her wedding being expelled with it.

Key Largo cut to a decibels-louder commercial for a 1-900-number phone sex line.

Seamus grabbed the remote control, lowered the volume and looked at C.J. "How was work?"

"Pretty dead for a Wednesday night. You'd better go to bed pretty soon or you'll never be able to get up in the morning."

He shrugged. Then he said, "There's something I want to tell you, C.J."

She stared at the cheap-looking women on the television screen, afraid to look at Seamus's face, afraid of what she'd see in his eyes. He had been quieter than usual lately, more withdrawn. What if he was already getting sick? What if he wanted to tell her that he only had a few months left? Or weeks?

She clenched the cigarette and took another drag.

"What is it?" she asked Seamus after a moment.

"I've been doing a lot of thinking, and I've made up my mind about some things."

"What . . . things?"

"How I want to live my life—whatever's left of it," he added.

She looked sharply at him, but couldn't read his expression.

He lit another cigarette off the one in his hand and said, "I don't want to waste any more time, C.J. I'm going to quit my job at WZZ, and I'm going to start working down at the AIDs center. I've been talking to Pete Peigh, my counselor there, and it's what I want to do."

C.J. nodded. She knew Pete. He had been the one who had given her the negative results of her own test.

"What do you think?" Seamus asked, watching her.

"I think . . ." She paused. "I think that you're right to want to have a career that means something. But are you sure it won't be depressing for you, being surrounded by— you know . . . ?" She trailed off uncomfortably.

"By people who have AIDs?" He gave a brittle laugh. "I'm surrounded by them now, C.J. A dozen of my friends and Chad—and hell, what about me? I can't escape it. I can't spend every day at some meaningless job that isn't doing anything positive except helping to put more money in a few rich bastards' pockets. I want to spend my time helping people . . . people like me."

C.J. reached out and squeezed his arm. "I think it's a good decision, Seamus. The only other thing is . . ."

"What?"

"What about money? A counseling job can't pay very much, and you can't just—"

"Money's not going to be a problem," he interrupted. "That's the other thing I wanted to tell you. When you get married, I'm going to move in with Chad. He inherited quite a bit of money when his lover died, including the apartment, which is paid for. I won't be paying rent, or anything."

"But, Seamus, just a few weeks ago, you said you'd never live with Chad."

"I know what I said, but . . . things change. I want to be with him. Every morning and every night for all the mornings and nights we have left. You never know when . . . you just never know," he finished quietly.

So far tonight, C.J. had only made ten dollars in tips. Razzles was always slow on Sundays, especially now that blustery November was here.

People would rather stay home on the couch and watch television—C.J. included. In fact, lately, she wondered what she was doing here.

Why wasn't she working a normal nine-to-five job like everyone else?

Why wasn't she with her fiancé, who was, at this very minute, cozy and comfortable in his studio apartment across town, watching some trashy movie-of-the-week and eating take-out Chinese?

C.J. knew exactly what David was doing because she'd just called him for the third time since her shift had started two hours ago. He'd chatted with her for a few minutes, but she could tell he wanted to get back to his moo shoo and the TV.

Who could blame him?

What she wouldn't give to be with him right now, instead of in this stupid bar, stepping around a sticky spot on the floor where a bottle of sour mix had spilled earlier.

And—uh-oh.

C.J. saw Jackie, the cocktail waitress, come out of the ladies' room, glance at her section of still-empty tables and head for the bar.

Great. Now C.J. would have to listen to yet another story about Jackie's wedding last month. For some reason—probably since C.J. was about to get married herself—Jackie assumed that she was interested in every last detail about her wedding.

She had already told C.J.—several times, in fact—what she had worn on every inch of her body, right down to the lacy satin panties that had cost over thirty dollars.

She had given her a complete rundown of what songs her cousin Lloyd, the deejay, had played at the ceremony.

And she'd related far more details than C.J. was comfortable knowing about the amazing sex she and her husband, Drew, had had on their wedding night.

As Jackie made her way over, tossing her long blond hair, C.J. considered dashing to the other end of the bar to escape.

But Steve, the other bartender, was hanging around down there. She'd already had two arguments with him tonight—one about abortion rights, and one about gun control—and she wasn't in the mood for another.

So she braced herself and waited for the inevitable.

"C.J., what's up?" Jackie asked, smoothing her short black uniform over her long, lean thighs as she settled on a stool. "How are your wedding plans going?"

"Good. I—"

"Did I tell you that I made my own garter? All you have to do is take a wide piece of white satin ribbon, and fold it in half. Then you..."

C.J. sighed mentally and tuned out Jackie's painstaking step-by-step instructions. The last thing on her mind was making a garter.

She had more important things to worry about.

Like Thanksgiving, which was this week. David's father, Fawn, Lauren and Andy were flying in that morning to spend the holiday with the Clarkes.

It wasn't that C.J. was concerned about David's family meeting her family. No, that part would be fine. Her mother and Fawn got along so well, it was scary. She knew her father and Bob Griffin would hit it off; Kyle and Andy would probably talk sports for hours; and who wouldn't love Lauren?

No, that wasn't the problem.

The problem was that she was scheduled to work on Friday and Saturday nights. Marty, the manager, had said he was sorry, but the nights following Thanksgiving were Razzles' busiest of the year. She could have Thursday off, but he needed her over the weekend, and that was all there was to it.

What was she going to do? David had been really upset when she'd told him, and her mother had been furious. Lila had kept insisting, over the phone, that there must be some way she could get out of working.

C.J. had wanted to say, *Do you think I'm thrilled about you guys and and David's family and David all spending the weekend together while I schlepp back into Chicago to work at some crummy bar?*

But she knew what her mother would say in response to that. Lila was upset about her being a bartender in the first place.

And anyway, Razzles wasn't exactly a *crummy* bar. It was actually a very *nice* bar.

But that wasn't the point.

It wasn't as though this job was worth the sacrifice. It wasn't as though C.J. needed to pay her dues and work her way up a ladder to...what? Head bartender?

Seamus's words echoed in her mind. *I don't want to waste any more time. . . .*

"C.J., are you even listening to me?" Jackie's voice cut into her thoughts. "You have this look on your face like you're a million miles away."

"Sorry. I'm listening."

Jackie looked dubious.

But after a moment, she shrugged and went on, "Okay, so you take your glue gun and your miniature silk rosebuds and you . . ."

Wednesday morning, C.J. was dumping clothes into the open suitcase on her bed when the doorbell buzzed.

Puzzled, she went down the hall to the security intercom. Who on earth could it be? David had said he was going to try to leave the office early so they could beat the holiday traffic out of Chicago, but she didn't expect him until at least noon.

And Seamus had already left town. He and Chad had flown down to Houston last night to spend Thanksgiving with Chad's family.

Maybe someone had pushed the wrong doorbell.

"Yes?" C.J. asked, pressing the talk button on the intercom. "Who's there, please?"

"It's Chris."

"Chris?" She raised her eyebrows. She'd almost forgotten that he was going to be in town. She pushed the button again and said, "Come on up!"

She opened the door and leaned out into the hall, listening as the elevator made its creaky ascent from the lobby.

Finally the doors opened and a familiar, lanky figure stepped out.

As he walked toward her, she noticed that he was wearing his usual uniform of torn jeans and a leather jacket. At first she thought that his dark hair was shorter than usual. Then she realized that it was longer—he was wearing it in a ponytail at the nape of his neck.

"Hi, C.J.," he said, giving her a hug.

"Look at you," she said, and playfully tugged his ponytail. "You're a regular long-haired musician now, huh?"

"I guess," he said, and she fleetingly realized that the usual teasing gleam was absent from his dark eyes.

"Come on in," she urged.

Chris stepped over the threshold. Only when he had set them down with a thud at her feet did C.J. notice that he had bags with him.

"What's that?" she asked, looking from the large, ragged-looking duffel and rectangular Macy's shopping bag to his expressionless face.

"That," he said, "is my luggage, and the present I bought for Madelyn. It's a china music box that plays 'A Time For Us.'"

"How sweet!"

"Yeah" was all he said. He stepped around the bags and walked past her, down the hall. "I need to use your bathroom, okay?" he called over his shoulder before he disappeared inside and closed the door with a sharp click.

"Sure," C.J. muttered, staring after him.

He came out moments later, and the first thing he said was, "I guess you're wondering what's going on."

"You could say that."

"Before I go into it . . . is it okay if I stay here for a few days?"

She blinked. "Sure, but . . . why? I thought you were going to spend Thanksgiving with Madelyn."

"Yeah, well, so did I. But when I showed up at her place this morning, I found out that surprising your girlfriend isn't such a good idea. Madelyn wasn't exactly thrilled to see me."

"She wasn't?"

"Would you be thrilled to see David if you had another guy sleeping in *your* bed?"

C.J. opened her mouth, then closed it. She was stunned. Quiet, serious *Madelyn* was sleeping with someone else? It was impossible to believe.

Chris stood there with his arms folded in front of him, glumly waiting for C.J.'s reply.

She finally found her voice. "Are you sure he wasn't just a friend?"

"Positive. She was wearing a skimpy little thing I bought her at Victoria's Secret, and she got all flustered as soon as she saw me."

"Oh, God, Chris…I'm so sorry. It must have been a bad scene."

"Yeah." He shrugged. "So, can I stay here?"

"You can, but are you sure you want to? I mean, tomorrow's Thanksgiving…. Wouldn't you rather be with your family? Your father lives in the suburbs, right?"

"Yeah, but we don't exactly get along. You know that."

"Well, can't you fly back to New York? David and I can drop you at O'Hare, if you want."

"Are you kidding? This is the busiest travel day of the year. Everything's booked. And according to my ticket, I have to stay over Saturday night. I'm stuck here."

C.J. had never seen Chris look so miserable. Her heart went out to him. "Look, Chris, why don't you come to Oak Hills with David and me? My family would love to have you, and—"

"Thanks, C.J., but no thanks. I'm not in the mood for some big family thing." He nudged his duffel bag with his toe. "I'll just stick around here."

"Well, I'll be back on Friday. Unfortunately, I'm stuck working over the weekend."

He looked up. "You still bartending at Razzles?"

"Yeah."

"I'll cover for you, C.J."

"You will?"

He shrugged. "Why not? It'll give me something to do, as long as I'm stuck here."

"Oh, Chris...that would be great!" she said excitedly. "I have to call David and tell him."

"Go ahead."

"I'll be right back," she said, trying to tone down her delight for Chris's sake. "Make yourself at home."

He shrugged. "Thanks."

She hurried into the kitchen and dialed David's work number.

For once, he answered his own line on the first ring. "David Griffin."

"Hi. Guess what?"

"C.J.? What?"

"I don't have to work on Friday and Saturday after all."

There was a pause. Then David said, "You don't?"

C.J. frowned. Was she crazy, or did he sound disappointed? "No, I don't."

"What happened?" he asked. "How did you get out of it?"

"It's kind of a long story," she said, conscious of Chris in the next room. "Someone's covering my shift for me."

"Oh." He hesitated. "Good."

"David, what's wrong with you? I mean, is it my imagination, or are you not thrilled that we can spend the whole weekend in Oak Hills with our families now?"

"No, of course I'm thrilled, C.J. It's just..."

Exasperated, she said, "Just *what?*"

"You'd better call your mother right away and tell her that you don't have to work now."

"I'm not in the mood to deal with my mother, David. I'll tell her when we get there tonight."

"You'd better call her now," he said again.

"Oh, for heaven's sake. Why?"

"Because she had planned a surprise shower for you on Saturday, that's why."

"She *what?*" C.J. shrieked.

"When you said you had to work, she decided to move the shower to Chicago. So unless you want two dozen of your closest friends driving all the way into the city on Saturday morning for no reason, you'd better call your mother now, C.J."

There was a long silence.

"C.J.?"

She couldn't answer him. She was speechless.

The indomitable Lila Clarke had struck again.

Eight

Was there anything more stressful than trying to act pleasantly surprised when nothing about a situation was pleasant *or* a surprise?

C.J. had reluctantly promised David that she wouldn't tell her mother he'd told her about the shower.

But even if she hadn't known, she probably would have picked up on the clues.

Lila and Fawn kept exchanging knowing smiles over the Thanksgiving dinner table.

Her father had snuck the punch bowl down from the attic.

Her mother had baked three dozen cream-puff shells and hidden them in the back of the refrigerator.

She overheard Lila asking Lauren whether she'd managed to find a quilt in "Clara Joy's colors." Alarmed, she'd wondered what her mother had decided her colors were.

When, on Saturday morning, Lila "casually" suggested that David and C.J. go out to "a nice, romantic lunch," she was tempted to refuse.

But the warning look from David made her sigh inwardly, shrug and say, "Why not?"

Now, as she and David walked up the driveway after lunch, she glanced over her shoulder at the line of cars parked along the street, and muttered, "I can't *do* this."

David squeezed her hand. "Sure you can, C.J. Just act surprised and smile nicely at everyone. Remember, they're here in your honor."

"I know," she said, feeling a twinge of guilt. "But, David, I *hate* all this hoopla and being the center of attention."

"Just think of it as good practice for our wedding day, then."

She paused at the foot of the steps leading to the deck. "I have an idea. Let's go back to the car and elope right now."

"Very funny."

"I'm serious."

"Move it."

She sighed and they started climbing.

C.J. stopped on the top step and looked at him. "Please don't make me do this."

"C.J., you're being ridiculous. This is a *party,* not major surgery. You'll have fun. I promise."

"Will you stay with me?"

He gave her a patient but unbending look and shook his head. "I already told you, I'm meeting your father, my father, Kyle and Andy down at the Moose Lodge."

"It's not fair. I'm not the only one who's getting married, here. Why do *you* get to shoot pool and drink beers while I suffer?"

"Don't be ridiculous. You're not going to suffer."

"Are you sure?"

"Of course I'm sure. Now come on," David said firmly. He gripped her elbow, opened the sliding glass door and ushered her into the kitchen.

She could see the corner of a bakery cake hidden in a paper bag on the counter, and she heard a muffled giggle.

Taking a deep breath, she followed David around the corner toward the living room, telling herself that she had no choice, so she'd just have to—

"Surprise!"

Pink crepe paper.

A mountain of gaily wrapped gifts.

Women of every shape and age, most of them in floral print dresses, and all of them chattering excitedly.

C.J. smiled weakly and turned toward David.
He had fled.

C.J. sat on the edge of the "throne" her mother had concocted out of a dining room chair draped in a pink sheet. She was surrounded by discarded wrapping paper and smiling so hard, her jaw and cheeks ached.

Thank God she was nearly finished opening gifts. It was becoming torturous to sit here in front of two dozen raptly attentive guests, trying to think of something other than "I love it!" to say about each present she unwrapped.

"Okay, here's the next one," her friend Tina St. John said, handing her a medium-size box wrapped in lavender-and-white paper stamped with umbrellas and the scrolled words *Showers of Happiness*.

"What beautiful wrapping paper," C.J. said, and saw her aunt Bess's pleased nod.

"Hold it up and smile, Clara Joy," her mother called from across the room, and snapped a picture.

C.J., blinking rapidly, removed the pink bow, and had to wait only a second before Fawn called, "Hand it over here, Clara Joy."

She was collecting every bow from every package, and busily taping and stapling them to a white paper plate.

When C.J. had asked her what she was doing, she'd just smiled and said, "You'll find out!" and the room was filled with knowing giggles.

She dutifully opened Aunt Bess's gift. Holding it up, she announced, "It's an electric juicer. I love it!"

"Now you can make David fresh juice every morning before he leaves for work," her grandmother chirped from the couch.

"Uh, right," C.J. said.

"Yeah, or David could make C.J. fresh juice," her friend Robin Alston commented. "After all, she works, too."

C.J. cringed. Not just because her job was a sore subject these days, but because she knew her grandmother wasn't going to let that comment go by.

Sure enough. "A man making juice?" Her grandmother snorted. "I wouldn't have let my Tony into my kitchen even if he had *wanted* to be there. It's the wife's job to make the juice."

C.J. saw Robin and Emily, who were sitting beside her, exchange a glance. She wanted to pull them aside and whisper that her grandmother tended to be a little old-fashioned. Yeah, sure. Just like Lila tended to be a *little* overbearing. But unfortunately, C.J. was stuck on this stupid throne with all eyes on her.

There was nothing she could do but hurriedly say, "Thanks for the juicer, Aunt Bess," and hand it over to Lauren, who sat on her right with a notebook. She was making a list of gifts so that C.J. could write her thank-you notes later.

Tina handed her another wrapped box that was suspiciously similar in shape and weight to the one she'd just opened.

Fawn promptly confiscated the bow.

Lila called, "Hold it up and smile, Clara Joy," and snapped another picture.

They were getting this gift-opening routine down to a science.

C.J. took off the card, pretended to read the long Hallmark verse intently and then checked the signature.

"This one is from Mrs. Noto," she announced, and looked around the room for her next-door neighbor.

The woman was wearing a tight smile.

C.J. saw why when she tore away the wrapping paper.

"An electric juicer!" She held it up and frantically she tried to think of something else to say. She glanced at Tina and saw the sympathetic look on her friend's pudgy face.

Lauren was wearing a similar expression.

"Uh, thank you, Mrs. Noto," C.J. said helplessly. "David and I really *love* fresh juice. We'll be drinking a lot of it, and, uh…" *Shut up, you idiot,* she commanded herself. "I love it," she finished lamely.

Mrs. Noto gave a grim nod.

Her grandmother said from the couch, "What's she going to do with *two* of those?"

Oh, God, please, no, C.J. thought.

But He wasn't listening, because her grandmother went on. "I don't even have *one.* I used to squeeze my Tony fresh orange juice every morning with these two hands."

Beside her, aunt Bess said, "Ma, it's not for orange juice. It's for other kinds of juice. Carrot juice, parsley juice—"

"*Parsley* juice? What kind of husband wants parsley juice before a hard day of work?"

C.J. handed the juicer to Lauren, who muttered, "Hang in there, C.J., you're almost through."

She gritted her teeth, gamely accepted another gift from Tina, and the process began all over again.

Finally, all the gifts were opened. The room was filled with chatter again, and a relieved C.J. was about to rise from her throne when Lila clapped her hands and called, "Ladies, can we have your attention for just another moment?"

The room fell silent, and C.J. thought, *Uh-oh.*

"I think my daughter, the guest of honor, has something she wants to say to all of you," Lila said, and prompted C.J. with a smile and a gesture that said, *Go ahead, make a nice little speech.*

At first, C.J.'s head was so filled with murderous thoughts that she couldn't think of a thing to say.

Then she managed to clear her throat, find her voice and start talking. "Uh, I just want to thank everyone for coming, and for the beautiful gifts. I love them all and I, um, hope you'll all be able to be at our wedding in a few weeks, and…thanks again."

Everyone murmured some variation of "Awww," and then the room was filled with applause.

C.J. smiled nervously, shot her mother a look that said, *Am I free now?* and made a move to get off the throne.

A hand clamped on her shoulder, forcing her back down. "Ah-ah-ah, you're not finished, Miss Bride-to-be!"

She looked up to see Fawn, brandishing the bow-bedecked paper plate. Her future stepmother-in-law announced, "Everyone, get your cameras ready. I've made this beautiful bonnet for Clara Joy to pose in." As she spoke, she plunked the plate onto C.J.'s head and tied the ribbon streamers under her chin in a loopy bow.

Everyone laughed and gathered around, flashbulbs flashed and C.J. sat there, a stiff smile pasted on her face.

David's words echoed in her head.

You're not going to suffer.

She made a mental note never to listen to him again, no matter what he said.

"Our wedding is going to be perfect," David said calmly, "and nothing your mother or my stepmother do is going to ruin it."

C.J. raised an eyebrow at him and said nothing.

"You'll see. All this worrying will be for nothing," he went on, stepping around a giant puddle on the sidewalk. "Stop making yourself crazy."

C.J. hesitated. Then she said evenly, "I'm *not* making myself crazy, David. I only mentioned that my mother called this morning and informed me that she had contacted the caterer and changed the menu we ordered to something 'a little more traditional.' Something 'easier to digest.' Something 'less fattening.' David, instead of Chicken Chaucer, she told them to serve plain broiled chicken breasts!"

She knew her voice was growing dangerously shrill in the quiet neighborhood street, but she couldn't seem to control it. "And she changed our julienne zucchini and spaghetti squash in butter-herb sauce to boiled peas. And—"

"C.J., calm down! What we serve isn't that important."

She stopped walking. "David, it's *our* wedding! We wanted Chicken Chaucer! We wanted julienne zucchini and spaghetti squash in butter-herb sauce!"

He just shrugged. "It doesn't matter."

"It matters to me." She stood there clutching the real-estate classified section against her chest, feeling as though she were on the verge of hysteria. "I wanted Chicken Chaucer! I wanted—"

"I know, I know." He stepped forward and put his arms around her. "C.J., the important thing is that we're getting married. In just a few weeks, you're going to be my wife. I'm going to be your husband."

"I know, but . . ."

But I wanted Chicken Chaucer.

She knew she should just drop the whole thing.

She'd been in an emotional frenzy ever since her mother had called this morning and dropped her bombshell.

C.J. had protested and argued and insisted until finally Lila had said, "Think about it, Clara Joy. You don't want to eat such a rich, heavy meal on your wedding day and look all bloated in your pictures. A lean entrée would make so much more sense."

Stung, C.J. had shut up—and hung up, without another protest.

Her mother had won.

Worse yet, Lila had managed to remind her in her usual oh-so-subtle way that she had not lost any weight and her wedding was looming ahead.

As if C.J. weren't aware of that fact.

As if she didn't wake up every day, look in the mirror and vow to fast from now until the end of December.

Then an hour later, she would catch herself eating something she shouldn't be eating, and she would hate herself. But she couldn't seem to stop. There was so much to worry about. Not just wedding details. No, that kind of stress, she could handle. It was the actual *marriage* stuff that was tricky.

Every time she thought about how happy she was, how lucky to be marrying a wonderful guy like David, a nagging little doubt invaded her mind.

Not a doubt that she loved him, or that he loved her. That, she knew.

A doubt that their marriage would last.

She couldn't stop thinking about all the shattered romances around her. She kept picturing her brother, Kyle, the way he had moped around all Thanksgiving weekend. And the gloomy expression on Chris's face when she'd arrived back at her apartment on Sunday afternoon.

What if, one day, she woke up and found that her marriage was over?

And then, besides the marriage worries, there was the problem with her career—or lack of one.

She had come to the realization that she hated being a bartender. She hated the hours, and she hated always feeling sticky and she hated waiting on drunks. She hated the condescending way some people treated her, and she hated herself for wanting to announce to everyone that this work was beneath her—that she had a brain and she'd been on her way to being a television producer.

Because, the truth was, she hadn't respected herself any more when she'd been working at WZZ. At least now she didn't have a psychotic, bitchy boss breathing down her neck, asking her to run personal errands. And the money she was making at Razzles was a hell of a lot better.

So what was her problem?

She couldn't do it forever. She had to figure out what she wanted to do next. But she couldn't figure it out because she had her wedding to worry about, and losing weight and her relationship with David.

She was a bride-to-be.

This was supposed to be the happiest time in her life.

Why was she so miserable?

David loosened his arms around her and patted her shoulder. "Come on, now, C.J. It'll all work out. You'll see."

She didn't say anything. She couldn't.

"Are you ready to go see that apartment? We're going to be late."

She sighed and found her voice. "Yeah, I'm ready."

"Good. This should be better than those two we looked at yesterday. It's the one with the eat-in kitchen, right?"

She consulted the circled ad in the paper. "Right. It also has a dishwasher."

"I have a feeling that this is going to be the place for us."

"I hope so," C.J. said as they started walking down the street again.

Yesterday, they had looked at two tiny, shabby dumps that had sounded positively palatial in the ads. Even the usually optimistic David had ruled them out on the spot. They had trudged back home to circle more ads in the newspaper and make more calls. This was the first place on today's agenda. The other two apartments they were going to see were on the sky-high end of their price range, but this first one was semiaffordable.

A few minutes later, they were standing in front of a three-story yellow house with a glassed-in porch.

"It *looks* nice," C.J. said hopefully, noticing the hanging plants and lace curtains in the windows of the first floor.

"It does. Keep your fingers crossed."

Together they walked up the stone steps and David knocked on the storm door.

A moment later, a pretty, middle-aged African-American woman appeared. She shivered as soon as she opened the door.

"Come on in. It's freezing out there!" she said, stepping back and reaching down and grabbing a small furry black thing that came hurtling from behind her. "No, Olive, you can't go out."

She scooped it into her arms, and C.J. saw that it was a cat.

"You must be Mrs. Talbot," David said, reaching out to shake the woman's hand. "I'm David Griffin, and this is my fiancée, C. J. Clarke."

"Nice to meet you. You can call me Janelle, and this is Olive. Come on up the stairs, and I'll show you the apartment."

She opened a door that opened off the porch, and they followed Janelle, still clutching a furiously meowing Olive, up a steep flight, past a landing and a closed door and up another flight.

Janelle balanced the cat in one arm, took a key ring from her pocket and unlocked the door at the top of the stairs. "Careful you don't hit your head. The doorway is low," she said over her shoulder to David.

He stooped, and C.J. followed him into the apartment.

"This used to be an attic," Janelle told them. She dropped the squirming cat, who promptly darted off into a corner behind a couch. "That's why the ceilings are sloped like that."

C.J. looked around the room. The floors were polished hardwood, the walls were whitewashed and there were interesting angles and nooks everywhere, thanks to the house's gabled roof.

"The couple who lived here is still in the process of moving out," Janelle said, gesturing at the boxes stacked in one corner. "Come on into the kitchen."

C.J. and David followed her through another low doorway. The kitchen was bright and surprisingly spacious. Someone had stenciled a border of red hearts on the sloping walls.

"Debbie did that," Janelle said. "She's a graphic designer."

C.J. assumed Debbie was one half of the couple who lived here. She wondered if she and her husband had moved in as newlyweds. There was a cozy table with only two chairs in the little nook by the window.

C.J. wondered if maybe Debbie and her husband were moving out because they needed more space for a family. She pictured a pregnant Debbie cooking supper for her husband at the little apartment-size stove. Then she thought of her grandmother and changed the image, picturing Debbie's husband cooking something for his pregnant wife, who would be sitting right over there at the table, reading a maternity magazine.

David walked over and opened the refrigerator, then checked the cupboards and the stove. C.J. could tell he was pleased.

"The bathroom is here," Janelle said, opening a door across the room.

C.J. and David peeked over her shoulder and inspected it. Small but functional. C.J. pictured her green toothbrush and David's yellow one hanging side by side in the now-empty holder.

She reached out and squeezed David's hand. He glanced at her and smiled.

She felt fluttery excitement.

This place wasn't huge, and the appliances seemed a little dated, but it was homey and cozy and she could imagine living here with David.

"Last but not least, over here," Janelle said, walking to another door, "is the bedroom."

C.J. crossed her fingers and hoped that it would be as perfect as everything else had been.

It was.

The room was small, but charming. There was a big brass bed covered with a wedding-ring patterned quilt similar to the one Lauren had given C.J. as a shower gift. Over the bed hung a painting-size portrait of a pretty dark-haired bride dancing with a handsome blond groom. Obviously, Debbie and her husband.

"Mind if we look in the closet?" David asked Janelle.

"Go ahead."

He and C.J. walked over and opened the door. The space inside wasn't enormous, but there seemed to be enough room. Of course, maybe that was because it was nearly empty right now. On one side of the closet hung a few summery dresses, and on the other were some lightweight suits.

"They've taken most of their things out of here," Janelle said. "I know they want to be out before the holidays, so you would be free to move in before the first of the month if you wanted to."

"That would be perfect. We're getting married on the thirtieth, and then we'll be on our honeymoon for two weeks. We'd love to be able to be settled before the wedding, right, David?"

"Right. Mrs. Talbot, would you mind giving us a few minutes to talk this over?"

"Call me Janelle," she said again. "And of course not. I'll wait for you downstairs. Olive? Here, kitty, kitty."

There was no response.

"Here, kitty." Janelle paused, waited and then shook her head. "That cat is always trying to get away. I'll come back up and get her later."

She left the room, and C.J. heard her starting down the two flights of stairs.

"What do you think?" she asked David.

"What do *you* think?"

"I think I *love* this place!"

He grinned. "So do I. Let's take it."

She bounced on her heels and reached over to give him a squeeze. "We're going to be so happy here, David! I'm getting great vibes. It feels like home, doesn't it?"

"Definitely." He hugged her tightly, then released her and looked around the bedroom again.

Debbie and her husband smiled contentedly down at them from the wall.

"Come on," C.J. said, catching David's fingers and tugging. "Let's go tell Janelle."

Together they headed down the stairs. C.J.'s mind was already filled with decorating ideas. They could put her bookshelves on the wall under the living room window, and she could hang the new T-Fal pots and pans her mother had given her from the hooks above the stove. . . .

Janelle was waiting for them in the glass porch at the foot of the stairs. "Well?" she asked expectantly.

"We'll take it," David said.

She broke into a smile.

"We love it," C.J. added. "It's the perfect place to start our marriage. Did the couple who live there now come in as newlyweds?"

"Glen and Debbie? Yes, they did. They were married about a year ago." Janelle paused as though she were going to say something else. Then she said, "I'll need the first month's deposit now, to hold the apartment, but you can pay the first month's rent before New Year's. Why don't you come on into my living room and I'll get the lease?"

C.J. and David followed her through another door that led off the porch into a comfortable room filled with books and plants.

C.J. decided that the living room upstairs needed lots of plants, too. Maybe David would put up some hooks so she could hang some in that windowed nook on the far wall. . . .

Janelle left the door open and said, "That way, Olive can get back in."

C.J. thought about the cute dormer window in the kitchen and wondered if she should hang curtains or just leave it to let in plenty of sunlight. . . .

"When do you think we'll be able to move in?" David asked Janelle, who was rummaging through a rolltop desk.

"Let's see . . . today's the fifth, right? Glen is moving the rest of his things on Saturday. And Debbie told me she'd be out by the fifteenth."

C.J. was jarred out of her decorating reverie. "They're moving *separately?*"

"Unfortunately, yes," Janelle said, glancing up briefly, then going back to shuffling through the papers in the drawer. "They're getting divorced. It's a shame, but—good, here's that lease. Why don't you two have a seat on the couch and we'll go over it?"

C.J. hesitated, her enthusiasm dribbling away.

Debbie and Glen, the smiling, glowing bride and groom from upstairs, were getting divorced.

Well, so what?

They were strangers.

Who cares?

C.J. and David walked toward the couch, where Janelle was waiting with the lease.

They were almost there when something streaked in front of them.

Olive.

The black cat had just crossed their path.

Great, C.J. thought glumly. *Just great.*

Nine

C.J. looked up from her seating plan diagram when she heard the apartment door slam. A moment later, Seamus walked into the kitchen.

"Hi," she said, stretching and rubbing her aching neck. She had been at this for hours. "How come you're home so early?"

"I gave my notice this morning," he said with a grin. "I felt so good all day that when four o'clock rolled around I decided what the heck? I left."

"Good for you. Congratulations."

"Thanks." He pulled out a chair and sat across from her. "What are you doing?"

"Making up the table arrangements for the wedding. You know, who's sitting where. It's a real pain in the butt. And I know my mother's bound to switch it all around anyway." She set down her pen and leaned back in her seat. "So tell me what they said when you told them you were leaving? I want to hear everything."

"Well, I told them I was giving two weeks' notice and that I'd work up until Christmas. I don't start my new job until the week after New Year's. So they were psyched that I was giving them enough time to replace me—unlike *some* people who quit on the spot."

C.J. shrugged. "I just couldn't take that place for another minute after they promoted that slimy Eve clone over me."

"Eve clone?"

"You know, the movie *All About Eve,* with Bette Davis? Where that sneaky little Eve person takes over everything?"

"Right. Well, guess what?"

"What?"

"I think that everyone at WZZ regrets what happened. That was mostly your boss's doing. Leonora didn't want to promote you and lose the best assistant she ever had."

"Of course I was the best assistant she ever had. I was the only one stupid enough to be her doormat without complaining."

"Not to her face."

"Right."

"Well, now that Leonora's been gone for a few months, you'd be surprised at how many people are willing to say that they despised her and they don't know how you put up with her for as long as you did."

"Really?" C.J. thought about that. She'd always sensed that some people in the office—like Seamus's boss, Dwight Horrigan—had sympathized with her. And no one had ever been brazen enough to defy Leonora and stick up for C.J.

"Really," Seamus confirmed. "Even Axel Riddance says it was a shame that we had to lose you."

"No way!" Axel was the producer who had been Bailey Norwiche's boss, and everyone knew he had pushed to have Bailey promoted so that he could hire a big-boobed bimbo to take his place. Sure enough, Seamus had reported that as soon as Bailey moved into the assistant producer office, the vacated production assistant spot had been filled by a cheerful, busty blonde named Skipper.

"C.J., you know what I think? I think that if you went in to WZZ and asked for my assistant producer spot, they would hire you back in a second."

"They would not. Not after the way I quit."

"Yeah, but your replacement did the same thing three months later," Seamus pointed out. "And the *next* assistant they hired for Leonora only stuck it out for six months because she had two kids to support and needed the job desperately. And then even *she* left. I think that was what made them finally sit up and notice that Leonora was the problem—not her assistants. That's why they fired her.''

"So you're saying that no one blames me?"

"I've been trying to tell you that all along, C.J. You never wanted to listen."

"Well, I didn't really care. I had left that place behind for good."

Seamus folded his arms, cocked his head and looked her in the eye. "But now you're changing your mind."

"About what?"

"About your career. Right?"

"What do you mean by that?"

"Come on, C.J., it doesn't take a genius to figure out that you're miserable bartending at Razzles."

She picked up her pen and seating chart again. "I am not."

"You complain about it constantly. Last night I heard you stomping around at 3:00 a.m. after you came home from work, muttering under your breath about some guy named Steve."

"Oh." C.J. wasn't about to tell Seamus that she and Steve had had yet another argument stemming from Steve's vehement antihomosexual politics. "I just had a bad night."

"Every night must be a bad night there lately, then. Because I can't remember the last time you didn't grumble all the way out the door on the way to work, and all the way to your room after you came home. Speaking of which, don't you have to start getting ready to go soon?"

She checked her watch and made a face. "I guess."

"See? Look at you! You don't want to do this anymore, C.J."

She hesitated, about to protest again. Then she shrugged and said, "You know what? You're absolutely right."

Seamus grinned and nodded. "I knew it."

"But I'm not sure *what* I want to do. I was so miserable at WZZ. And how could I go crawling back there?"

"You wouldn't be crawling back. You'd go in as an assistant producer. You'd have an office. You wouldn't be working for Leonora. You'd be working for Dwight, and he's a great boss. He always liked you."

"That's true." She thought about it. "But, Seamus, even if I did want to go back, what about my wedding?"

"What about it? They wouldn't need my replacement to start until after the holidays anyway. Your wedding is before New Year's."

"But David and I are flying to California for our honeymoon. We're spending two weeks there."

Seamus shrugged. "Maybe you can cut it short. Or maybe they'll let you start later. If they had to hire someone totally new, it would take at least two weeks to train the person. You've already worked there. You know the ropes."

C.J. caught her bottom lip in her top teeth and frowned. Then she said, "You're right. I'm going to go for it. I'll call Dwight first thing in the morning."

"Good." Seamus grinned. "I know they're going to hire you."

"What if they don't?"

"They will."

C.J. pushed back her chair and stood. "I have to go get ready for my shift."

"Want me to take over with the seating arrangements? I *am* your man of honor."

She smiled. "I wish you could, but you don't know half these people. Hell, *I* don't know half these people."

"Why don't you just arrange the tables randomly? That would make for an interesting party."

"Sure, and what if you and Chad wound up seated with my grandmother?"

"We'd charm her."

"You don't know my grandmother." C.J. headed for the hallway. "Thanks for the tip on WZZ, Seamus."

"No problem."

In her room, she changed out of her sweats and into the black pants and white blouse that were her uniform for Razzles.

She wondered how it would feel to never have to mix another drink or have another argument with politically incorrect Steve again.

It would feel wonderful.

Yes, she was going to call Dwight first thing tomorrow.

And if she got the job, all she'd have to worry about was doing the stupid seating chart.

And finishing the million other things she had to do before the wedding.

And losing forty pounds in the next three weeks.

And buying Christmas presents for a dozen people.

And making sure she and David stayed married for the rest of their lives.

No problem.

C.J. was rolling out cookie dough for Christmas cutouts when the phone rang on a Wednesday afternoon.

She guiltily dropped the piece of dough she'd been about to pop into her mouth, wiped the flour off her hands and went over to answer it.

"Hello, is this C.J.?" a masculine voice asked.

She recognized it immediately.

Dwight Horrigan.

It had been a week since she'd interviewed with him. She'd already resigned herself to the fact that she probably wasn't going to get the job. Even Seamus had admitted that he didn't know what was going on, but it wasn't a good sign that no one had called her yet.

Now C.J.'s stomach lurched crazily and she tried not to sound giddy as she said, "Yes, this is C.J."

"Dwight Horrigan here, C.J. I know you've probably been wondering why I haven't contacted you yet, but things have been crazy around here. I've been producing a Santa Claus exposé that's really been overwhelming.''

"A Santa Claus exposé?''

"A ring of department store Santas is involved in some pretty shady business. A real racket. It's a crying shame, what they're getting away with.''

"I'm sure it is,'' C.J. said absently as she frantically wondered why Dwight was calling.

This doesn't mean you've got the job, so calm down, she told herself. *He could just be calling to let you know they hired someone else.*

She eyed the bowl of raw cookie dough on the counter.

And if they did *hire someone else, you have permission to scarf down that entire ball of dough.*

Dwight cleared his throat and said, "But anyway, the reason I'm calling is to offer you the position.''

It was all she could do not to shriek into the phone. She paused for a moment, trying to calm down, and said in a businesslike tone, "That's great.''

Dwight went on for a few moments, discussing the salary, benefits and bonus incentive. C.J. said *uh-huh* and *I see* in all the right places, but all she was thinking about was that she couldn't wait to tell David!

And she couldn't wait to walk out of Razzles and never look back!

And she couldn't wait to—

Uh-oh. She'd forgotten something.

When Dwight paused for a moment, she tentatively said, "Um, can I ask you something?''

"Sure.''

"It's about my wedding. I think I told you in the interview that I'm getting married the week after Christmas...''

"You sure did. Congratulations.''

"Thanks. Um, I was wondering when you'd need me to start the job. Because we had planned to take a honeymoon....''

"I see. For how long?''

She winced and said, "Two weeks?"

There was a long moment of silence.

She squirmed and eyed the cookie dough.

Then Dwight cleared his throat and said, "I think we could manage without you for that long."

This time, she couldn't hold back a happy little scream. "Thank you so much, Dwight."

"No problem. We hate to lose Seamus, but we'll be glad to have you back here, C.J."

"I'll be glad to be back," she said truthfully. *Glad to have some career goals again.*

She called David as soon as she'd hung up with Dwight. He was in a meeting, so she asked his secretary to have him call her as soon as possible.

Then she went back to the cookies.

She rewarded herself for getting the job with a tiny little nibble of dough.

Then she thought that it was a big deal, and she deserved a bigger reward, so she took a bigger nibble.

And then, because she was so excited, she ate another chunk.

And another.

And by the time David called back, the bowl was empty.

But she was so happy, she didn't care—until she walked into her room later and saw her wedding dress hanging there.

Her jubilation instantly gave way to despair. Her wedding was less than two weeks away now. Who was she trying to kid?

She wasn't going to be a thin, beautiful bride. It was too late. She'd failed.

There was nothing to do but throw herself on her bed and sob.

"So, C.J., how does it feel to be having a last hurrah?" Jessica asked across the table.

It was the night before Christmas Eve, and since David's friends were holding a stag party for him, C.J.'s friends had decided to take her out on the town, too. Becky had even come all the way from Iowa for the occasion. They were starting at Razzles, and C.J. got a secret satisfaction out of being waited on by Jackie.

C.J. raised an eyebrow and set down her margarita. "I wouldn't know, Jess. I expect to be having lots of 'hurrahs' as a married woman."

Jessica, Becky and Robin laughed at that.

Emily didn't.

Jessica, who never missed a thing and didn't know that Emily had been separated from her husband, asked, "What's up, Emily? You're the only married person here. Are you trying to tell us that marriage isn't all it's cracked up to be?"

C.J. tried to kick Jess under the table.

But it was Becky who flinched and said, "Ow!"

"Oops, sorry," C.J. said.

Jessica had rested her chin on her hand and was obviously waiting for a reply to her question.

Emily set down her seltzer and lime. "It depends on the marriage," she said in her quiet way. She paused, and added, "I think C.J. and David are going to be fine."

"Hey, we forgot to drink a toast to them!" Robin said, lifting her drink. "Here's to a long and happy life together."

Everyone clinked glasses, and C.J. breathed a sigh of relief when the conversation turned to speculation about where David's friends had taken him in their rented limousine. Seamus and Chad, who were in on the plan, had refused to spill a thing about it.

"Jake was the mastermind behind this whole thing," Jessica said. "But all he would tell me before he left was that they were going to get David wrecked."

"They can try, but David's not much of a drinker," C.J. said, shaking her head. "Besides, we have to be up at seven."

She and David were driving home to Oak Hills, and they had to be there in time for the annual Christmas Eve brunch at her aunt Bess's.

Jessica looked dubious. "If anyone can talk David into having a few too many beers to celebrate, it's Jake. You know, I'll bet they're at that new stripper bar, Babes in Boyland. Jake's been there quite a few times since it opened last month."

Becky looked shocked. "He has? Doesn't that bother you?"

Jessica shrugged and tossed her blond hair. "Why should I worry about a few strippers? It's harmless."

But C.J. thought her laugh that followed seemed brittle.

"How *are* things with you and Jake?" Becky asked.

"Fine." Jessica fiddled with the straw in her mineral water, then said, "Oh, who am I trying to kid? Things are not fine. They're horrible."

"What's wrong, Jess?" C.J. asked.

"Jake's a workaholic, for one thing."

"You just said he goes out to stripper bars. He can't be *that* busy," Robin pointed out.

"He always goes with clients. And when he's not entertaining them, he's working late at the office. Or so he says. I can't remember the last time he was home to have dinner with me."

"Marsh used to be that way," Emily said. "Now he's home every night by six-thirty. He even gives Joseph his bath and puts him to bed before we eat."

"Really? Maybe Jake and I should have a baby, then."

Emily shrugged. "It's a lot of hard work."

"That's what people are always saying about marriage," Becky said. "It makes you wonder why anyone bothers to— sorry, C.J."

"It's okay." She took the last swallow of her margarita. "I wonder the same thing myself," she heard herself admitting.

"You're not getting cold feet?" Robin asked.

C.J. set her empty glass down and raised her hand to flag Jackie, who was waiting on the next table. Then she said, "I'm not getting cold feet, but I don't think anyone could be on the verge of vowing to spend the rest of their life with one other person and not have a teeny little doubt in the back of her mind."

"You have *doubts?*" Becky asked. "About you and David? Oh, come on. You guys are perfect together."

"I know, but..." She trailed off as Jackie appeared at their table.

"Another round, ladies?" she asked.

Becky and Robin were only half-finished with their drinks and shook their heads. Jessica, who was the designated driver, asked for another Evian.

And Emily, who had already gone to the pay phone twice to call Marsh, pushed back her glass and said, "I have to get going home, actually. Joseph's been running a temperature, and I'm worried about him."

"Are you sure, Em?" Robin asked, as Jackie headed back to the bar. "You look like you need to relax. Marsh can probably handle things for a little while longer, don't you think?"

"He probably could, but I just..." She shrugged and stood. "C.J., you have a wonderful Christmas. And if you need any help with last-minute wedding stuff next week, call me."

"I will. Don't forget, the rehearsal is at six Friday night. Do you have the directions to the Moose Lodge?"

"If I don't, I'll call you."

Emily was doing a reading at the ceremony. So was Robin. And Becky and Jessica, along with Tina and Lauren, were going to be bridesmaids.

After Emily left, the conversation turned to the wedding. Jessica wanted to know what kind of flowers they were going to be carrying.

"A single white rose with baby's breath," C.J. said.

Jess nodded her approval. "Elegant."

C.J. knew her friend, who had impeccable taste, also liked the dresses she had selected for the bridesmaids. They were going to be wearing plain black velvet three-quarter-length dresses. Naturally, Lila had thrown a fit at the idea of black bridesmaid attire, but C.J. made sure the dresses were all ordered before she'd told her mother about them. That way, it was too late for anything to be changed.

"I can't wait to see your gown, C.J.," Becky said. "Did you get it back from the alteration place yet?"

C.J. hesitated. "Uh, actually, I haven't brought it in yet."

Jessica stared at her. "Your wedding is a week away! What are you waiting for?"

How could C.J. tell her she was waiting to see if she could miraculously transform herself into the perfect, *thin* bride after all?

Jackie appeared just then with C.J.'s second margarita. "Here you go," she said, setting it down. "I think Steve made it pretty strong, so look out."

C.J. slid the glass closer and took a big swallow. It was potent enough to burn going down, but when it landed it made her feel pleasantly warm and fuzzy.

Were margaritas fattening? she wondered belatedly.

"David still doesn't know you're wearing his mother's dress, does he?" Robin asked.

C.J. frowned, trying to focus. "No. I think I'm going to surprise him on our wedding day."

"He'll probably be thrilled," Becky said.

"I wouldn't be so sure." Jessica tilted her head to one side, and said in her blunt way, "David's mother is dead, remember? He might feel like C.J.'s invading a part of his life where she doesn't belong."

C.J. set down her drink and stared at her friend. How had Jessica managed to hit the nail so squarely on the head?

The alcohol must have loosened her tongue, because she heard herself saying honestly, "Actually, that's part of what's bothering me, Jess."

"What is?"

"That I have no idea how David will react to my wearing his mother's dress. That I have no idea how he feels about a lot of things. I mean, sometimes, I feel like I don't even know him. But I guess it's no big deal, right?" She gave a nervous laugh.

Her three friends were staring at her. None of them cracked a smile.

"C.J., what do you mean you don't know David?" Robin asked. "You've been together for over two years, right?"

"Right." She picked up her glass again and sipped her drink. "But that doesn't mean anything."

"Of course it does," Becky said. "You guys have built a relationship."

"But I know what she means," Jessica said. "Sometimes I feel like Jake is a stranger. I look at him and think, how could I be with someone who would do something like...well, like whatever he happens to be doing that's bugging me."

C.J. frowned and stirred her foamy lime-green drink. She wasn't exactly thrilled to have her relationship with David compared to Jessica's with Jake, since it wasn't exactly blissful these days.

"I think that as long as two people love each other and are honest with each other, they can work things out," Becky said conclusively, and sipped her wine.

Honest with each other.

"That's the other thing," C.J. said. "Honesty. Are you supposed to tell the person you love *everything?*"

"Yes," Becky said without hesitation.

Jessica and Robin looked tentative.

Then Jess said, "No. I think that if you tell someone everything, you risk hurting them. Like, I would never tell Jake that I hate the gold bracelet he's getting me for Christmas."

Robin asked, "How do you know what he's getting you?"

"I found it in his drawer when I was snooping the other day."

"Jessica!" Becky chided. "You were sneaking around looking for your gifts? He obviously wanted to surprise you."

"I wasn't trying to find my gifts. I was looking for something else, and I just happened to find the bracelet." She made a face. "I know it was expensive and everything, but it just isn't me."

"What *were* you looking for?" C.J. asked.

Jessica paused, then shrugged. "Nothing. I mean— something. Anything, I guess, that would give me a clue about why he's been so distant lately."

"You mean, like, some woman's phone number, or a lipstick-stained hankie?" Robin asked.

"Maybe. Who knows what he's up to? Maybe it's nothing. Or maybe it's something, and I'm better off not knowing."

C.J. thought again about her fling with Dig. "Do you really think so?"

Jessica shook her head. "I don't know. I mean, if he were cheating on me, and I found out, I might feel like I should dump him. And I don't want to do that."

"That doesn't make sense," Becky said, frowning. "Why wouldn't you want to dump him if he was sleeping with someone else?"

"Because I love him," Jessica said simply. "And I don't want to give him up, for whatever reason."

"What about if he *had* cheated on you, like a year ago, but it was over now? What if it happened even before you moved in together?'' C.J. asked. ''Would you want to know that?''

''What good would that do?'' Jessica asked. ''It would only make me feel lousy, and if it's over, who cares?''

''I don't agree,'' Robin said. ''I'd want to know if my boyfriend had cheated on me. It would mean I couldn't trust him. And without trust and fidelity, what do you have?''

Becky nodded. ''I agree.''

C.J. lifted her margarita and drained the rest of it.

Then she made up her mind. The minute David came back to her apartment after the party later, she was going to tell him about Dig. That way, she could clear the air and know they were going into this marriage without secrets between them.

C.J. was still awake at five in the morning when someone opened the door of her room. She had been waiting up for David, going over and over how she was going to tell him about Dig. She had decided to tell him casually, as if it were no big deal. After all, it wasn't. Was it?

''Honey, I'm home,'' David's voice slurred, and then he giggled.

Giggled? David?

The light went on, and she blinked at the sudden brightness. It was a few moments before she could really see the sight in the doorway.

Seamus and Chad each had one of her fiancé's arms draped over their shoulders. David's hair was messy and his face was bright red. He was wearing a big, loopy smile and a button that said Kiss The Groom.

''Oh my God,'' C.J. said.

''Where do you want him?'' Chad asked.

C.J. was about to say the couch when she remembered that Becky was spending the night. ''Uh, I guess I have no choice. My bed,'' she told them.

''Come on, David,'' Seamus grunted. ''Walk.''

But they had to drag him the few steps to the bed. They turned him around, then let go. David fell backward and landed faceup beside C.J.

Seamus grinned at C.J. "He's all yours, you lucky gal."

He and Chad headed for the door.

"I love you guys," David said tipsily, waving his hand at them.

"We love you, too, darling," Seamus said dryly, blowing David a kiss. He closed the door as he and Chad left.

C.J. looked down at David.

"How was your party?" she asked cautiously.

"Jus' great," he said happily. "I had lots o' beers."

"I can see that."

He reached up blindly and tugged at her arm. "How 'bout a li'l kiss?"

"David . . ."

"C'mon."

She sighed and leaned over. When she pecked his lips with her own, she was almost blasted away by the overpowering fumes of liquor.

"David, you have to go to sleep now," she said, pulling back as he sloppily tried to prolong the kiss. "We're leaving in about two hours to drive to my parents' house, remember? It's Christmas Eve."

His eyes widened. "It *is?*"

"Yes."

"I love Christmas!"

"Good."

"And I love *you.*"

"Good."

"You love me, too, right?"

"Right. Now go to sleep, David. I'm going to turn off the light." She got off the bed and walked over to the switch.

Behind her, David murmured again, "I love you, C.J. You're gonna be my wife."

She turned off the light and stood there in the darkness for a moment.

Then she heard a snore from the bed.

He was already asleep.

C.J. sighed, shook her head and climbed into bed beside her husband-to-be.

After a moment, she tenderly brushed his hair back from his face. He didn't stir.

She sighed, snuggled into his warm back and closed her eyes.

Ten

"Seamus?" C.J. called as she unlocked the apartment door and stepped inside.

Kyle was right behind her, wearing his oldest jeans and a paint-splattered sweatshirt, and carrying a stack of collapsed cardboard boxes and a role of heavy packing tape. It was the Wednesday after Christmas, and he had risen predawn to drive a rented U-Haul into Chicago to move C.J. from her old home to the new one she would share with David.

The apartment was silent and, in the early December morning hours, still shadowy.

As soon as C.J. flicked on a light, she realized that not only was Seamus not here—he had already moved out.

There were bare nails where his collection of Ansel Adams prints had hung beside the door, and his Oriental area rug, which C.J. had always hated, was gone.

Now she realized with a pang that maybe it hadn't been so bad, that stupid rug.

Maybe living here hadn't been so bad, either.

She turned to her brother. "I guess Seamus must have moved out yesterday. Knowing him, he probably didn't want to be the last one to leave because he'd have to make sure everything was clean." She gave a hollow laugh.

Kyle's smile turned into a yawn. "Got any coffee around here, C.J.? I could use some caffeine before I start lugging boxes up and down those stairs. Figures the elevator's out of order today."

"It was out of order most of the time I lived here," she said. "I won't miss climbing all those flights...."

Yes, she would, she realized.

And she'd miss waking up in the morning to Seamus's off-key singing in the shower. She'd miss the bedroom she'd had here for three years, with its uneven floorboards and the big paned window that looked into an apartment across the way where an old woman lived alone, crocheting and watching soaps all day, every day. She'd miss the creaking, groaning sound the pipes made early in the morning, and she'd miss the blasting steam heat that made it necessary to open all the windows on cold winter days.

"C.J.?" Kyle prompted.

"Huh?"

"Coffee? I asked you if you had any. You zoned out on me. Looks like you could use a caffeine jolt, yourself."

"Oh, sorry. Uh, come on into the kitchen and we'll—" She stopped halfway there. "I forgot. The coffeemaker was Seamus's."

Kyle shrugged and yawned again. "No problem. I'll run down to that place on the corner and get us some. You take it black, right?"

She did when she was trying to lose weight. But now, with her wedding only three days away and every last pound of her still intact, why bother? Besides, the place on the corner made lethally strong coffee. It was too early in the morning to pour that undiluted acid into her stomach.

"I'll take two—no, three creams and two sugars," she told her brother, and reached into the pocket of her ripped jeans for a ten dollar bill. "Here. Get yourself a doughnut or something, too."

"Hey, thanks. You want one?"

"No tha—" She hesitated. The day ahead was going to be a grueling one, both physically and emotionally. She *deserved* a doughnut. "I'll take one of those glazed apple fritter kinds," she told her brother. She almost added, "But don't tell Mom."

It was what she'd always said to Kyle when they were growing up and C.J. ate something she knew Lila wouldn't approve of. Loyal, sympathetic Kyle had never told. In fact, during a finicky-eater phase he'd gone through, he'd sneak his food onto her plate so Lila wouldn't make him stay at the table until he finished. C.J. had always told herself that she was doing her brother a big favor by polishing off his unwanted chicken drumsticks or mashed potatoes or creamed spinach, never admitting that the portions her mother placed on her own plate were never enough. Growing up, it seemed she had always been hungry.

Some things never change, she thought, acknowledging her empty stomach, which was rumbling now in anticipation of that crispy-gooey apple doughnut.

Here she was, three days away from her wedding, and she was inevitably going to be a fat bride.

"I'll be back in, like, two minutes," Kyle told her slipping back into his heavy winter jacket and heading toward the door.

"Okay. Be sure to get a few napkins. We ran out last week, and we're going to need whatever paper towels are left to clean up the place before we leave today."

"No problem." Kyle closed the door behind him with a click.

He was such a good kid, C.J. thought, walking down the hall and into her bedroom. She knew he had better things to do, being home on Christmas break, but he'd volunteered to help her move. On the other hand, he'd seemed kind of lost these past few days, and C.J. knew he was still missing Tammy. Maybe he was grateful to have something to do.

David couldn't move her because he was working all week, saving his vacation days for their honeymoon. C.J. hadn't seen him since he'd left at dawn on the twenty-sixth to drive back into the city. The only time they'd been alone together all weekend was when they'd driven to Oak Hills early in the morning on Christmas Eve. And David had been so hung over then that C.J. had driven, and he'd slept the entire way. As soon as they arrived at her parents', they'd been plunged into a whirlwind of holiday chaos.

Now, C.J. wouldn't see David until Friday afternoon. He was picking up his family at O'Hare, and would arrive in Oak Hills in time for their wedding rehearsal.

He had called her several times the past few days from the office, but there had been no opportunity for private conversation. Either his other line would start ringing, or Lila would interrupt C.J. with one of her endless wedding details.

And anyway, even if C.J. found the opportunity to have a quiet conversation with David, what would she say to him?

Would she make her confession about Dig?

Would she ask David, point-blank, if he was as anxious as she was?

Not just about the wedding, but about their marriage?

Would she ask him to reassure her that he would always be there for her, that nothing would ever come between them, no matter what?

And even if he did, would she believe him?

How could she? There were no guarantees. Everywhere around them, there was evidence that love didn't always last forever, even when you had been sure it would.

C.J. sighed and surveyed the bedroom she had left a few days ago.

There were boxes and suitcases everywhere—she'd done most of her packing over the past two weeks. But still, there were items to collect from the rest of the apartment—her towels in the bathroom, her CD collection, her cookbooks, baking equipment and drawers full of kitchen utensils....

She'd better get busy.

But suddenly she just didn't want to do this.

Any of this.

She didn't want to pack, and she didn't want to move.

She wanted to go back to her life the way it had been.

Why did everything have to change?

"I'm not ready," she whispered, and was startled to find that she was crying.

Stop it! she scolded herself. *You love David. You want to be with him. It's time to move on, to start your new life.*

But still, she stood wrapped in nostalgia, unable to budge.

She could hear echoes of Jessica's shrieks when her morning shower turned suddenly scalding or freezing.

Once again, she felt Becky's reassuring pats on her arm when C.J.'s life seemed to be falling apart.

And saw Chris McGuire standing in the doorway, flashing that lazy grin of his.

She closed her eyes and breathed Seamus's heady scent—cigarette smoke and expensive cologne.

And she let the unexpected waves of regret wash over her.

None of those people were going to be a part of her daily life ever again.

From now on, it would be her and David, on their own.

And as much as she loved David, as much as she wanted to live with him, she couldn't help feeling an overwhelming sadness for the part of her life that was over for good.

C.J. stood in her old room at her parent's house, studying her reflection in the mirror. She was wearing the new black dress she'd bought just for tonight—for her wedding rehearsal and the dinner the Griffins were hosting afterward, at the Claypool House restaurant on Main Street.

She had carefully finger-combed her long curls, and had painstakingly applied her makeup. In the mirror, her charcoal-liner-rimmed eyes stared solemnly back at her, and her round face was pale despite the blusher she'd smoothed along her cheekbones.

She looked the way she felt—utterly composed and detached.

She'd been this way ever since she'd first opened her eyes this morning and thought that this was it—the day before her wedding. Now, in just a few minutes, David and his family would arrive, and the series of events leading up to the big occasion would be set in motion.

Why wasn't she feeling . . .

Something?

Why wasn't she elated, or scared out of her mind?

She turned from the mirror and slipped her feet into her too-tight new black pumps. Then she calmly put on the new antique heart-shaped filigree gold and pearl earrings David had given her for Christmas.

Again, she looked in the mirror.

Nothing.

It had been the same when she'd tried on her wedding dress for one last time earlier. She had stood here, expecting to see herself transformed into someone breathtaking and magical—a bride.

Instead, she'd seen her regular old chubby self in a nice white dress. That was all.

From beyond her closed bedroom door, she heard the doorbell ring and, from the master bedroom on the other side of her wall, Lila's excited "Tom, they're here! Can you get that? I'll be right out, as soon as I've finished spraying my hair."

She heard her father's rumbling reply, and then his heavy footsteps going down the hallway. Then the living room was filled with chattering voices, and her mother's heels were tap-tapping along the hall as she hurried to greet everyone.

C.J. stood riveted in her room, not wanting to go out there yet, not ready to take the plunge and get things officially underway.

She just needed to be alone for a few more minutes. . . .

There was a knock on her door.

She sighed. "Come in."

She half-expected to see her mother poking her head in, but it was Lauren's face that appeared. "C.J.—wow, you look great!"

"Thanks . . . so do you." She saw that her soon-to-be sister-in-law's face and belly had grown considerably rounder than they'd been a month ago. Lauren looked happy and glowing—the way *a bride* was supposed to look, the way C.J. should look right now.

She let David's sister hug her, and asked, "How was your flight?"

"It was fine—on time, no turbulence. I don't think the little guy liked it much, though," she added, rubbing her stomach. "He kicked me the whole time."

"He?"

"Actually, we don't know yet, but I hate saying 'it.' We decided not to find out what sex the baby is after all. I'm dying to know, but Andy's really patient about the whole thing. He says we should wait and be surprised when the baby's born. Meanwhile, I'm dying of curiosity."

"I'd be like you," C.J. told her.

"And David would be like Andy, of course. Calm and collected, as usual. Although, if I didn't know better, I'd say that your groom seems a little out of sorts today. He forgot where he parked the car at the airport, and we had to lug our bags—including Fawn's *three* giant suitcases—all over the parking garage until we found it."

"You're kidding. That's not like David," C.J. said.

"Well, he *should* be a little jittery. He's getting married. In fact, so should you. Why do you look so calm? I was a basket case before my own wedding."

C.J. shrugged. "I don't know."

Lauren looked past her and caught sight of the wedding dress that hung on the back of the open closet door. It was wrapped in yards of plastic from the cleaner's.

"Oooh, there it is. How did it come out? Did they get out that tiny stain on the skirt?"

"Uh-huh."

"Wait till David sees you. He still doesn't know you're wearing Mom's gown, does he?"

"No. How do you think he'll react?"

"I think he'll be thrilled."

"You do?"

Lauren shrugged. "Sure."

C.J. detected a hint of uncertainty. "You're not positive, though, right?"

"You know David, C.J. He's usually totally predictable, but every once in a while, like with that parking garage thing, he catches you by surprise."

"Yeah" was all she could say to that.

"And speaking of David, we'd better go out into the other room. He can't wait to see you. Are you ready?"

C.J. inhaled deeply, then exhaled.

"I'm ready," she said.

She followed Lauren down the hall.

As soon as she stepped into the living room she was enveloped in a flurry of hugs and excited chatter. She worked her way from her future in-laws to David, who had been standing at the far end of the room, talking to Kyle.

C.J. was almost disappointed to see that he looked like his usual self—good-natured and relaxed.

"Hey, I missed you all week," he told her, catching her in his arms and giving her a big hug.

She looked up into his eyes, begging him to read what was in hers.

Take me away from here, David. I need to be with you, to talk to you . . .

But he just grinned down at her, and then he was letting her go, and Fawn was dragging her off to see the earrings she'd found to go with her purple sequined mother-of-the-groom dress.

And C.J. realized that she and David wouldn't be alone together until after it was all over. . . .

After they were married.

She sighed inwardly, then forced her attention to Fawn and her sparkly earrings.

The banquet room of the Moose Lodge was filled with people when C.J. walked in.

She spotted Father Barney and Rabbi Krantz over in one corner, comparing notes on the ceremony. Seamus and Chad were sitting off to the side on folding chairs with Jessica, Jake and Becky, and all of them were laughing hysterically about something. In a quiet corner, Robin was happily bouncing little Joseph on her hip while Emily and Marsh hovered protectively. Tina St. John, who taught music at Oak Hills High, was seated on the bench of the baby grand, chatting with Marge Olnauer, the wedding pianist. Grandma was barking instructions to the women from Lila's garden club as they arranged ivy over the rented *chuppah*.

C.J. just stood inside the doorway and looked around, suddenly struck by the fact that everyone who mattered most to her in the world was in this very room at this very moment.

She glanced over her shoulder at David. She wanted to share her realization with him, but she couldn't see his face. It was blocked by the enormous silk flower arrangement Lila had asked him to carry in from the car.

"Clara Joy, why are you lagging back there?" her mother asked, appearing and grabbing her arm. "You're the bride! We can't get started without you."

She had no choice but to allow herself to be dragged across the room to the *chuppah*, casting a longing glance back at David, who was wandering around with the flowers.

Father Barney, clad in faded jeans, a Notre Dame sweatshirt and sneakers, walked over with Rabbi Krantz. "Speak of the devil," the priest said jovially. "Here comes the bride now. We were just wondering when you were going to show up and get things underway."

"Well, here I am," C.J. said with a brief smile. "Mom, I'd like you to meet Rabbi Sam Krantz."

"It's a pleasure to meet you, Rabbi," Lila said graciously.

"And Father Barnabas Myer."

"Father Barney," he corrected with a grin. "How's it going, Mrs. Clarke?"

She saw her mother's eyes widen. C.J. could tell she was thinking, *You're a priest?*

But Lila managed to wipe the shock off her face and say simply, "Nice to meet you . . . Father."

"Where's the groom?" Rabbi Krantz asked, looking around.

"He's right over there, putting that flower arrangement on the table," C.J. said, pointing.

"On what table? Oh, no! It doesn't go on *that* table! Excuse me—I've got to stop him," Lila said, and rushed away.

"Looks like your mother's a little high-strung," Father Barney observed dryly.

"Mother-of-the-bride Syndrome," the Rabbi said.

"No, she's always that way," C.J. told them.

"Well, you're looking very relaxed for a bride-to-be," Rabbi Krantz said.

"Everyone keeps telling me that." C.J. shrugged. "I'm fine."

"Good. Stay that way, and everything will go smoothly. Are your father and the Griffins here?"

"Yes," C.J. said, looking around. "That's David's father over there in the vestibule, wearing the navy blue blazer. My dad is the one next to him, in the dark suit. And, let's see . . . David's stepmother is over there—the one in the fuchsia dress who's arguing with the coat-check man."

Both the rabbi and Father Barney watched for a moment as Fawn stamped her foot and brandished her fur coat at the nonplussed man behind the counter.

"Mother-of-the-groom Syndrome?" the rabbi asked hopefully.

"Nope," C.J. told him. "She's always that way."

"You must *really* love that David a lot," Father Barney said with a teasing smile.

"I really do," C.J. said, nodding.

As if on cue, David showed up at her side and slipped his left hand into hers while shaking the rabbi's and Father Barney's hands with his right.

"Hey," he said, giving C.J. a peck on the cheek. "Everyone's waiting. Are you ready to get this show on the road?"

She paused for the slightest moment before saying. "Yup, I'm ready."

Eleven

C.J. had been awake since three-thirty in the morning.

She had gone to bed at midnight, but hadn't drifted off until after one-thirty.

Which meant that she'd had about two hours of sleep.

Before she'd finally dozed off, and after she'd awakened, she had restlessly thrashed about in her bed, commanding herself to sleep.

You can't be exhausted on the most important day of your life.

Close your eyes.

Think relaxing thoughts.

Yeah, right. There were no relaxing thoughts to be found in these hours before her wedding.

What if the light flurries that were predicted turned into a raging blizzard?

What if the limousine her father had arranged for broke down on the way to the ceremony?

What if she tripped and went sprawling on her way down the aisle?

But it wasn't just the horrible *what ifs* that kept popping into her head. No, even worse than imagining all the nightmarish possibilities was C.J.'s nagging feeling that something was missing.

Something important.

She kept wondering, as she tossed restlessly in the dark on her too-soft girlhood mattress, what David was doing.

Probably sleeping soundly.

He hadn't seemed outwardly nervous at the rehearsal or the dinner that followed, but then, David never did.

He had appeared to be his usual calm and logical self the whole night. Not that C.J. had spent much time with him. They'd been seated next to each other at the dinner, but Fawn and Lila had commanded most of the conversation.

And then the speeches had started. First Andy, the best man, stood and gave a witty prewedding toast. Of course, Seamus, not to be outdone, had followed suit with a long-winded tale about the evolution of C.J.'s relationship with David. Then, of course, Lila had her say, followed by a teary oration from Fawn about weddings in general.

Then C.J.'s father had stood and, in an uncharacteristically choked-up voice, had told about how happy he and her mother were that their daughter had found someone who would "love her as much as Lila and I have loved her." He'd said it with his hand resting on his wife's shoulder, and naturally, her mother had cried.

After that, it seemed, everyone wanted the floor.

C.J. knew she should be honored and touched and amused by the tributes from her family and friends. But it was as though she were watching the action from behind a soundproof glass. Beside her, his arm draped casually across the back of her chair, David had laughed and nodded and commented. She'd gone through the motions, but somehow, nothing had been reaching her.

Her face had felt stretched out of shape from so much forced smiling by the time the dinner was over. That was when Andy, Jake, Kyle and the other groomsmen had whisked David away. C.J. had time to briefly peck him on the lips before he was gone, presumably to have, according to Jake, "a couple of beers with the boys."

C.J. knew there was no danger of a repeat of David's performance at last week's bachelor party. He had promised to be tucked into his bed at the Oak Hills Inn by a reasonable hour.

And, knowing David, he had been.

As C.J. lay watching the milky winter dawn finally seep through the windows of her room, she realized there was no going back to sleep now. She might as well get up and be the first one in the shower.

She slipped out of bed. The house was still chilly, but she could hear familiar creaking, clicking sounds as the heat kicked on. Apparently, everyone was still asleep. She went down the hall to the bathroom, and spent nearly a half hour under the steamy hot spray.

She'd been hoping the shower would wake her up, but she emerged and realized that now she was sleepy. Her eyes stung and her shoulders ached, and she knew that if she went back to bed, she would fall right to sleep.

But she couldn't do that. Her hair was wet, and if she slept on it, it would be squashed.

Back in her room, she stood wrapped in her robe and debated getting ready so soon. She could put on sweatpants for a while. But on the other hand, what was she going to do? Watch television? Read a magazine?

What did other brides do to kill time on their wedding days? She should have asked Emily.

Restlessly, she made her bed, then wandered over to peek out the window. The streetlights had gone out, and the frosty December air swirled with fluffy-looking snowflakes. It was wet snow, the kind that would coat everything in a heavy layer of white now, but might melt into a sloppy mess later.

For a few minutes C.J. watched it drifting lazily toward the already-covered ground.

Then she turned away from the window and her eye fell on the white wedding dress, still wrapped in its layers of clear plastic.

She paused only a moment before making up her mind.

First, she took out her quilted floral bag and carefully made up her face, using extra concealer under her tired eyes. She took off her robe and rubbed rose-scented lotion all over, then squirted on some perfume.

Then she put on the lacy white silk high-waisted French-cut underwear—the "something new" she'd bought in Marshall Field's lingerie department last week. She had a matching white camisole, too, but when she'd tried on the gown with it last night, she'd realized she needed more support if she didn't want her boobs drooping to her waist.

So, reluctantly, she put on her plain old D-cup cotton bra, then slipped the camisole over it. There. Not *too* bad. And besides, she'd needed "something old" anyway.

Next came the sheer off-white hose—control top, of course. She remembered to slide the cream-colored satin garter with its navy ribbon trim—"something blue"—up her leg. She hadn't told Jackie that she'd bagged the make-your-own garter idea. Lila had bought this one at the local bridal boutique and stuffed it into C.J.'s Christmas stocking.

C.J. ran her fingers through her air-drying curls, fluffing them, and then picked up the simple headpiece she'd chosen. It was just an ivory-colored hair bow with a wisp of illusion veil attached. She clipped it firmly to the back of her head and stepped back to check her reflection in the mirror. She had so much hair that it didn't feel like it was going anywhere, but she anchored it with a few bobby pins just in case.

She stepped into her simple satin pumps, and remembered to tuck a lucky penny into the right one.

There.

Now all she needed was the "something borrowed."

She walked over to the waiting dress and began to carefully peel away the layers of plastic.

Finally the dress was unwrapped. She looked at it, admiring the rich, creamy silk. And for the first time, she wondered about David's mother.

What had her wedding day been like? How had she felt in the moments before she'd taken this dress off the hanger and stepped into it? Had she been nervous? Jittery with excitement? Afraid?

C.J. pictured Sandra Goldstein Griffin, seeing her not as the middle-aged woman in the framed photo David kept, but as the young bride she'd glimpsed in the wedding picture in the Griffins' attic.

Someday, would C.J. and David have a daughter who might want to wear this dress?

Could David's mother have suspected that she wasn't going to live to see her own daughters and son get married?

Maybe. Her own parents hadn't been alive on Sandra's wedding day. Her father had died before she'd even been born, and the breast cancer that had eventually killed Sandra had taken her mother's life when Sandra was a teenager.

Just as she, herself, had died when David was a teenager...

That was when it hit C.J.

That was when she understood everything, all at once.

David.

And the reason he had insisted on having this Jewish ceremony.

It was a tribute to his mother.

Suddenly, C.J.'s stoic, detached reserve was gone. All the emotion that she'd been holding at bay came rushing over her, and she was crying. Hard. And rocking back and forth, her fingers reaching forward to clutch the old silk of the dress.

She understood the pain that David was keeping inside. She glimpsed the part of him that he couldn't share with her—not in words, anyway.

She sobbed for the little boy who had lost his mother, and for the mother who had been forced to say goodbye to her son too soon, much too soon.

And she realized now why David didn't talk about what it had been like after his mother died.

She realized how devastating the changes must have been for him, and for his sisters, and for his father.

She remembered what Lauren had told her—about how David had heard his father sobbing every night after Sandra's death.

She thought about something else.

About what her father had said during his toast last night—about *how* he had said it, with his hand on Lila's shoulder, smiling down into his wife's teary eyes.

She heard her grandmother saying, "I used to squeeze my Tony fresh orange juice every morning for fifty-three years with these two hands."

She imagined Lauren, her belly swollen and her face glowing, with Andy ever at her side, clutching her elbow and looking at her tenderly.

And she heard Seamus. "I want to be with him. Every morning and every night for all the mornings and nights we have left. You never know..."

C.J. wiped at her teary eyes. Her mascara must have smeared all over, but it didn't matter. Not right now.

She took a deep breath, then reached for the dress. Carefully she slid the heavy fabric from its hanger, and lowered it with a whispering *swish*.

She stepped into the skirt, then put her arms into the sleeves. It took her a long time to fasten every round fabric button up the back, but she worked patiently.

When she was finished, she lifted the rich folds of the skirt and walked across the room to the full-length mirror. What she saw in her reflection startled her. She didn't look like ordinary C.J. Not anymore.

Her cheeks were flushed, her eyes were sparkly with anticipation and there was ... well, a *glow* about her.

She looked like a *bride*.

A bride who was about to marry the man of her dreams.

A bride who believed in forever.

Outside, the winter sun sparkled on the pristine landscape, every tree decked in delicate ice crystals that glistened in the light like millions of diamonds.

Inside, the room was hushed, waiting.

Then David spoke, his voice trembling but true. "I, David, take you, C.J., to be my wife. I promise to be true to you in good times and in bad, in sickness and in health. I will love you and honor you all the days of my life."

He looked deeply into her eyes as he uttered the age-old words, his right hand clasping hers, and his tender gaze and his strong, sure touch enveloped C.J. in warmth and love.

She had felt it the instant she had stepped shakily onto the end of the white runner and seen him waiting there under the *chuppah,* handsome in his dark tux, his sandy hair carefully combed, his freckled face flushed and scrubbed and eager.

And in that moment, as she'd taken the first step toward him on her father's arm, seeing David's expression change from expectant to startled to deeply moved as he recognized the dress she was wearing, she had stopped feeling that something was missing.

There was nothing missing.

There were no secrets between them—none that mattered.

Now there was only love—deep, true love—and a mutual commitment to go wherever life would lead them—together.

And now it was her turn.

C.J. took a deep breath and began, her voice clear and strong.

"I, C.J., take you, David, to be my husband. I promise to be true to you in good times and in bad, in sickness and in health. I will love you and honor you all the days of my life."

Then she smiled and closed her eyes as her husband's lips came down over hers to seal their vows for eternity.

* * * * *

MONTANA Mavericks™

Stories that capture living and loving
beneath the Big Sky, where legends live
on...and mystery lingers.

This July, don't miss the exciting conclusion with

COWBOY COP
by Rachel Lee

Clint Calloway's orderly life turned chaotic after he
learned of his true parentage—and discovered his
explosive desire for the gorgeous rookie assigned as his
new partner. Dakota Winston was dangerous, all right,
and the last distraction Clint needed—because he was
on the verge of breaking the biggest case that ever hit
Whitehorn, Montana....

Only from **V**™ *Silhouette*® where passion lives.

MAV12

WESTERN *Lovers*

Stories by your favorite top authors with romantic Western settings and lots of cowboys, babies, reunited lovers, marriages of convenience and much more!

In July, look for these great titles:

CARVED IN STONE by Kathleen Eagle
"Ranch Rogues"...hard to tame, but easy to love!

Sexy Sky Hunter is a full-blooded Sioux as rugged as the Rocky Mountains he calls home. And when he meets Wyoming newcomer Elaina Delacourte, he's determined to give her some lessons about the land...and love!

SOMEONE WAITING by Joan Hohl
"Hitched in Haste": They bargained for marriage but not for love!

Royke Larson wanted a child and a wife was only a means to that end. But saying "I do" with sultry Stacy had him thinking less about a marriage of convenience and more about a marriage of *forever!*

Don't miss each and every WESTERN LOVERS title...all you love in romance—and more!

HARLEQUIN® Silhouette®

WL795

Bestselling Author

Introduces you to the woman called

Everybody loves Red—whoever she is. A haunted
teenager who defied the odds to find fame as a top model.
A pretty face who became a talented fashion photographer.
A woman who has won the love of two men. Yet, no
matter how often she transforms herself, the pain of Red's
past just won't go away—until she faces it head on....

Available this July, at your favorite retail outlet.

As a Privileged Woman,
you'll be entitled to all these Free Benefits.
And Free Gifts, too.

To thank you for buying our books, we've designed an exclusive FREE program called *PAGES & PRIVILEGES™*. You can enroll with just one Proof of Purchase, and get the kind of luxuries that, until now, you could only read about.

BIG HOTEL DISCOUNTS

A privileged woman stays in the finest hotels. And so can you—at up to 60% off! Imagine standing in a hotel check-in line and watching as the guest in front of you pays $150 for the same room that's only costing you $60. Your *Pages & Privileges* discounts are good at Sheraton, Marriott, Best Western, Hyatt and thousands of other fine hotels all over the U.S., Canada and Europe.

FREE DISCOUNT TRAVEL SERVICE

A privileged woman is always jetting to romantic places. When <u>you</u> fly, just make one phone call for the lowest published airfare at time of booking—<u>or double the difference back!</u> PLUS—

you'll get a $25 voucher to use the first time you book a flight AND <u>5% cash back on every ticket you buy thereafter through the travel service!</u>

LOOP-PP3A